Stories From The Chicken Foot House

Tina Jackson

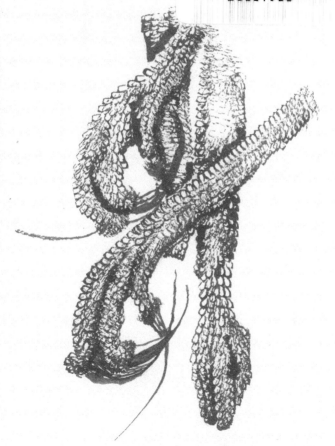

Illustrations By Andrew Walker

FIRST PRINTING, September 2018.
Harry Markos, Director.

Paperback: ISBN 978-1-912700-15-8
eBook: ISBN 978-1-912700-16-5

Book design by: Ian Sharman

www.markosia.com

First Edition

CONTENTS

THE GIFT OF A FLAMING SKULL

I once was Vasilisa
Walking through the forest
Looking for light

Now I'm Baba Yaga
My chicken-foot house
Dances with me

STORIES FROM THE
CHICKEN FOOT HOUSE

There is no reason why the stories I am going to tell you should not be true. And here is the first one.

In a village on the outskirts of a forest so deep that the souls of the people who got lost in it were said to howl to travellers to turn back, there once lived a young girl who dreamed of flying away, to a place where there were no mountains, and no trees, but only pretty dresses and handsome young men. And dancing. She was very fond of dancing. Her name might have been Lydia, or it might have been Zara, or it might even have been Vasilisa, but she was as pretty as the day and as full of dreams as nighttime.

One winter's day, when the darkness lasts until lunchtime and comes back to swallow the world at tea-time, all the women of the village took their baskets and walked to the edge of the forest to look for things to eat. 'Here,' said Zusanna, the stepsister of Lydia, or Zara, or Vasilisa, or whatever it was that she was called. 'We have hungry children to look after and you have none. So go ahead of us into the forest, and look for light so that we have more time to find food for our children, who will die of starvation if we cannot feed them.'

So Lydia, or Zara, or Vasilisa, walked into the woods without knowing where she was going. 'You are a good-for-nothing girl,' called Zusanna. 'Don't come back until you have found the light. There is not enough food to waste on a girl who has nothing to bring us.' And Zusanna added: 'Don't start daydreaming and wander from the path.' Because, as we have said earlier, the woods were very deep, and as we have not yet mentioned, full of wild creatures. Not just foxes and badgers, but wolves and bears. And some say other things too, but I wouldn't know about that.

Lydia, or Zara, or Vasilisa promised that she wouldn't leave the path, and wouldn't come home until she had found the light. And because she was scared of Zusanna, who often pinched her with fingers that were as sharp as her tongue, she set off into the woods. But although she was looking for light, her head was full of a handsome young wood turner who she might have seen walking through the village. And the handsome young wood turner might just have smiled at her because, as we have said, she was very pretty. So when she heard the chirping of a bird that sounded exactly like a line of music from a dance, she wasn't thinking about her step-sister's warning not to stray from the path.

'Come with me,' the bird's song seemed to say. It was such a pretty tune that she followed it deeper and deeper into the forest, not looking where she was going.

She followed the pretty notes until she reached the edge of a clearing, and by then the music of the bird's song had stuck so fast into her head that she

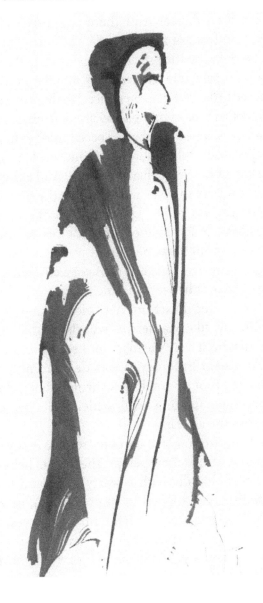

wanted to dance. And there was this wide-open space in front of her.

So she forgot that she had been sent into the forest to look for light, and skipped gaily into the clearing, and started to dance. But as she danced, the birdsong changed to another tune, and Lydia, or Zara, or it might have been Vasilisa, stopped as if she had been turned to stone.

Because right there in front of her was the strangest house she had ever seen. And although the weak winter sun was fading below the trees and the darkness was falling, Lydia, or Zara, or maybe it was Vasilisa, could make out that the reason the house was so strange was because it was mounted on two huge, scaly feet, just like those of a chicken. And the chicken foot house was dancing.

With her heart in her mouth and her eyes spinning like Catherine wheels, Lydia, or Zara, or maybe it was Vasilisa, looked around and saw that a bent little figure was descending from the chicken foot house. It was shrouded in a cloak and carrying a flaming skull, which lit its bearer's way across the clearing.

'Who are you, that dares to trespass in my garden? This is private property.' The voice belonged to a cross old lady with a warty nose, and teeth like needles. She stopped in front of Lydia, or Zara, or Vasilisa, and peered at her with bleary eyes.

"What do you want?'

'My step-sister sent me to look for light,' faltered the girl.

'Did she now? And I suppose she was hoping that you would get lost in the forest and never come back,' grumbled the old lady. 'And then she could give your share of the food to her children.'

'How do you know?'

'I know all the stories.' The old lady sounded as if she was boasting. 'I'm in some of them. And you, quite obviously, don't know enough of them. You don't know who I am, do you?'

'I'm very sorry but I don't.'

'I fly around in a pestle and mortar. Aren't you scared of me?

'Should I be?'

'And I eat children. Did you know that?'

'I didn't. But I'm not a child, so hopefully you won't eat me.'

'Don't be too sure of it. You'd make a lovely stew.'

'I don't think I would actually. I'm a bit scrawny because there's never enough food to go around. My step-sister Zusanna's much better coated.'

'Is she now?' The old lady's eyes gleamed and as she smacked her lips her needle teeth glowed yellow in the gathering darkness.

'She's the one that sent me here. So I'd better not stand here all night talking or she'll never let me hear the end of it. I don't suppose you could…'

'What, give you some of this?' The old lady waved the flaming skull in a wide arc in front of the girl's face. 'If you'd read the stories you'd know you'd have to earn it. I'd set you impossible tasks and only after you completed them would I allow you to go back to your old life, carrying a flaming skull through the forest.'

'If you gave me some light, I could show you where Zusanna lives.' Lydia, or Zara, or Vasilisa, may have been young, and she may have had a head full of dreams, but she was far from stupid. And the old lady was strange, but much less scary than her step-sister. 'That flaming skull would give her the proper heebie-jeebies. Serve her right. She's such a witch.'

'You're a bit of a madam, aren't you?' The old lady gave the girl an assessing look.

'And maybe instead of setting me tasks, I could help you round the house and you could tell me stories.'

The old lady thought about it for a moment and then nodded.

'You're brighter than most of the others that come this way, I'll say that for you. Wanting this, wanting that, weeping and wailing. Gets on my wick. At least you've got a bit of spirit about you. As for stories, you need to find your own. But if you come inside with me, we'll get you started.'

And with that, Baba Yaga linked arms with Lydia or Zara, or maybe it was Vasilisa. And lit by the flaming skull, they made their way across the clearing to where the chicken house, hopping from foot to foot in an excited little dance, was waiting to welcome its new guest.

ROCK'N'ROLL DREAM TOUR

You really have to want to find the car park tucked behind the back of the derelict turpentine warehouse in Vauxhall. You won't find it on Google Maps and it's not in the A to Z either.

But if you happen to be in the vicinity, you might notice that every Wednesday and Friday morning, a raggedy band of pilgrims make their way through the confusing labyrinth of tunnels and underpasses beyond the station to hitch a ride on the Rock'n'Roll Dream Tour.

They come from all walks of life but every one has the look of a seeker about them. A quester. Someone who wants to walk off the beaten track. Someone who's looking for more than a guided tour with the opportunity to hand over £12.99 for a branded mug and a stop-off at a public toilet reeking of chemical freshener.

There's no set start time for the Rock'n'Roll Dream Tour but the word gets round that if you're late the bus won't wait, and the pilgrims tend to turn up early, just after the 9am commuters have logged in for the daily grind. There's nothing to do and nowhere to sit in the car park so the punters loiter around, wander up and down, vaping and drinking coffee and peering at their phones, although the networks won't pick up a signal. This is weird in itself because London is one of the most connected cities in the Western hemisphere.

Time to zoom in a little. Who have we got today? There's Miki, Ikuyo and their teenage daughter, who is called Yoko. All the way from Nagasaki and now waiting patiently, unaffected by the thin drizzle because they're wearing sensible waterproofs. Even though he's got his hood up, you can see Miki is sporting a Beatle haircut, round glasses and carefully trimmed facial hair. Ikuyo looks expressionless but she's concentrating hard on remembering the steps of her belly dance class's latest routine, which she's missing learning because of this family holiday. Yoko is shaking her iPhone, anxious because she can't get a signal, which means she can't catch Pokémon.

Watching the Japanese family and extravagantly not talking to each other, Greg and Gary are both wondering if the row they had this morning about adoption versus surrogacy marks a milestone in their relationship, or its tombstone. Their natty clothes are slightly soggy.

And now there's a shift. If there were a theme tune it would be *Ghostriders in the Sky*. Everything speeds up. You can feel the fritz of tension in the air.

A dirty old white transit van careens into the car park and, braking, lurches to a sudden halt. Miki, Ikuyo, Yoko, Gary and Greg all duck to avoid the scattering gravel.

The front left-hand passenger door clunks open.

The first thing anyone sees is a battered military boot emerging from the footwell. But look at the side of the van. It's thick with spattered grime, though which the words 'Captain Rock's Rock and Roll Dream Tour', painted by hand, are clearly visible.

Up in the sky, sunlight breaks through the cloud and a mass of tiny rainbows, a faceted jewel around each drop of mizzling rain, surrounds the vehicle.

And Captain Chris Rock makes his entrance by catching his boot on the frame of the door and falling out of the van.

'Sorry about that. Got a bit of a head on me. Big night last night. Ah fuck it.'

As he picks himself up and bows from the waist all eyes are drawn to an extraordinary figure: part pirate, part punk; part showman, part shaman, and every inch the one-time rock star.

'Roll up, roll up, everyone aboard. Let's get this show on the road. Captain Rock, at your service. Behind the wheel, that's Mama, my other half of the last twenty-five years. The old ball and chain, the trouble and strife. That'll be thirty nicker apiece, ladles and jellyspoons, which is to my mind a fair exchange without a hint of robbery considering the marvels I am about to lay before your very eyes. Yeah, cash. I don't do cards. Apple Pay? Fuck it. We can pull into the garage if you're running short.'

The Captain is resplendent in a well-worn leather coat and a collapsible top hat with its brim decorated with feathers, a bird's skull and an array of laminates emblazoned with the words 'Access All Areas'. He swaggers to the rear of the van and heaves open the back door, revealing a stained mattress, two old

blankets, a broken down amplifier, some screwed-up newspapers, a roll of gaffer tape, a knackered Adidas bag and the bottom half of a drum case.

'In you get.'

The punters look at the back of the van, and at each other. Surely they can't be expected… it's 2018, after all, and this is some kind of joke, and retro's all very well but this is hardly what you'd call roadworthy, let alone sanitary, and any minute now a clean mini-bus will appear in the place of this… relic…

Miki has been learning English for years to prepare him for this holiday of a lifetime. 'There is nowhere to shit.'

'Yeah, I know, sorry about that, we're going to stop off at the nearest Costa though, Mama needs a coffee and I could do with a… Nah, I get it. This is rock'n'roll, man. You think we had our own seats, when we were on the road? Back of the van, that's where you sit. In you get.'

Gingerly, Miki and Ikuyo clamber in and perch on the edge of the mattress. Gary and Greg climb in next and ostentatiously sit as far away from each other as possible. This was meant to be so much fun, thinks Greg. Revisiting our indie disco days in 2004. I thought he looked like the lead singer from Bloc Party. I thought he looked like the lead singer from Franz Ferdinand, thinks Gary. And now we're here. Not speaking to each other on a dreadful mattress. I don't even want to think where the stains came from.

They way they have positioned themselves means there is no room for Yoko.

Captain Rock hauls himself into the back of the van and arranges the drum case behind the front seats. Then he invites Yoko to get in through the front passenger seat and settle herself inside the case.

It's a perfect fit. She looks up from her iPhone and smiles delightedly.

'He flamingo.'

Time for a change in the soundtrack. Outside it may be 2018 but in the van Captain Rock presses the button on the old-fashioned in-car cassette player and a warped, crackly version of Canned Heat's *On the Road Again* fills the air. For the first time we notice Mama, though we can't really make out her face because it's obscured by long hair, horn-rimmed spectacles and a trilby hat. Captain Chris Rock holds out the wad of notes he has collected from the punters, and without taking her eyes off the road, she stretches out a jewelled yellow hand for the money and secretes it in the folds of her clothing.

The soundtrack cuts out and there is an awkward extended silence punctuated only by the sound of crunching gears and wheels scrabbling on gravel as Mama cranks the van though a 17-point turn to get it out of the car park. In the process, the mattress slides down the back of the van. Miki, Ikuyo and Gary manage to keep their seats, but Greg rolls off. When he picks himself up, there's something unpleasant on the sleeve of his expensive jacket.

Gary casts a concerned look in his direction but Greg ignores him. The Captain fishes under the passenger seat and proffers a grimy towel. Greg takes it gingerly and drops it by the side of the mattress without using it.

Finally the van is out of the car park.

'Right.' The Captain swivels round in his seat and eyeballs the punters. His eyes would be a startling blue if they weren't so bloodshot, and there are black lines around them, which might equally be dirt, or last night's slept-in eyeliner.

'Let's get this show on the road. I gave my soul to rock'n'roll more years ago than you lot have had hot dinners, gave it my all, had a few hits, more than my fair share of misses, and I'm still out there doing it. Every Thursday night at the Red Lion. And if you need any more qualifications than that I got this badge.' He points to a chipped 'school prefect' pin on the lapel of his leather coat.

The Captain's face falls as his witticism fails to raise even the faintest of smiles from his audience. But showman that he is, he rallies.

'Now, you may not believe me, but there is good medicine to be had for those that step this way, my friends. I am no purveyor of snake oil and you will have to take my word for it that this may look like an ordinary – in fact, I can see from the looks on your faces, I wasn't born yesterday – low-rent form of transport, but it is in fact the perfect vehicle to transport you on this journey into the parts of rock and roll that other tours do not reach. Because the tour van is one of the foundations upon which the church of rock and roll is built. And if you believe, with all your hearts and souls, then I will show you marvels beyond compare, because that is the true meaning of rock.'

'Liverpool? Cavern Club?' Miki can't hide the excitement in his voice.

'Nah, mate, out of our way. And everyone there thinks they're a comedian. No, ladies and gentleman, the tour van, where you are now ensconced, is the first part of your initiation into the on-the-road experience. Because where would rock and roll have been without the wheels to get it to the punters? And this, in fact, is my van, in which my band – a Stonesy combo going by the moniker of The Justified Sinners – take our music to the masses.'

The Captain gestures modesty but proudly around the van, and manages to catch Ikuyo with the back of his hand.

'Sorry babe, sorry, I've had a bit of a problem with my peripheral vision ever since Roger our bass-playing lummox whacked me round the bonce with his instrument back in '83. I haven't done you a mischief have I?'

Ikuyo doesn't understand his words but she realises that he didn't mean to hurt her and smiles politely. In her head she's back in the dance studio in Nagasaki, trying to remember if it's camel, camel, maya, shimmy or if there's a hip drop she's missing.

She'll be so behind the others when she gets back and there's a hafla with a visiting teacher from Turkey the week after she gets back.

'Ah, rock and roll. You give it your soul, and it gives you everything in return because in rock'n'roll, anything can hap… WATCH IT BABE.' The Captain is interrupted in his speech as the van collides with a bollard and kangaroos to a sudden halt. Greg is catapulted off the mattress for the second time. Mama grinds the gears a few times and the van shudders back into life. Gary takes out a packet of tissues and silently passes them to Greg. Their hands touch briefly but they both jerk away from the contact. The silence is broken as The Captain sparks up and inhales noisily on a roll up. Gary coughs pointedly. Greg still smokes sometimes, which Gary isn't happy about, but if they're going to be a family he knows it's not fair on a child. Though whether that's still even an issue after this morning is a question in itself.

'Okay, okay, elf and safety. Rightio.' The Captain winds down the window and flicks the cigarette into the oncoming traffic. The window refuses to wind back up. After a moment, Ikuyo takes a beanie hat out of her bag and pulls it over Yoko's windswept hair. Yoko shakes her off, and points her phone to where a Pikachu is waiting to be captured.

The Captain, well into his spiel, eyeballs the punters.

'Right. Rock'n'roll. It's a broad church, but round here's a bit of a pilgrimage site I've got to say. If you look over there you'll see Soho, which is where a lot of musicians used to hang out and play gigs. The Marquee was down there, before it closed down, and then it was over there, on the Charing Cross Road – done quite a few gigs there myself – only it isn't any more. Down that road there's Dean Street, where a lot of musicians buy kit. How do you know when the stage is level? The drummer drools out of both sides of his mouth at once. I got loads of drummer jokes. Over there was a venue called The Astoria, where I've also played, and there was a musicians' pub quite near it called The Royal George, only that's gone too.'

'We paid £30 each for this.' Gary and Greg say the same thing at the same time, without looking at each other. Shyly, they both glance at each other and smile when they catch each other's eye.

The van stalls again just before the traffic lights change.

'Bit more left hand babe. I lost me licence owing to a little Jack Daniels-related incident on the A642 during what we'll call my lost period, or I'd be behind the wheel myself, but this way I can give you my full attention. Now, as we head up to North London, we'll be passing near one of rock'n'roll's most important landmarks.'

'Abbey Road,' breathes Miki.

'Nah, waste of space mate, though I once found an old shoe there. No-one said it didn't once belong to George Harrison so I got £90 for it on eBay.'

'Rooftop concert.' Miki looks as if he's going to burst into tears. 'John Lennon.'

'John Lennon is dead my man.' The Captain looks more closely at Miki and his expression alters. 'Of course, my friend. No problems. We'll stop off there so you can pay your respects.'

'Live forever,' says Miki softly.

'Now, Oasis I can do without. Never liked that band. In fact I once kicked the singer. But yeah, Mama, we'll leave the heartland for a detour via Abbey Road if you'll be so kind.'

Mama pokes a button on the cassette player. The wonky strains of *Magical Mystery Tour*, further warped by the terrible quality of the tape, flood the van. The van judders into life and the mattress slides across the van floor. This time it's Gary who wobbles and nearly loses his seat. Greg reaches out a hand to save him. Gary takes it gratefully, making Greg think how much his heart would break if he never held that hand again, before the violent lurch as the van moves off throws them apart again

Mama hits several bumpers as she backs the van at an angle into the nearest parking space to the most famous zebra crossing in the world. The Captain courteously ushers his passengers out of the Transit, helping Yoko to clamber out of her drum case, before reclining, one booted foot on the floor, the other propping himself at knee-height against a lamp-post.

'You lot have a nosey around,' he bellows. 'Mama? I'm leaning on a lamp-post. It's on the corner of the street and everything. In case you should pass by.'

The van's occupants look at the zebra crossing. Gary and Greg dutifully snap it on their smartphones. Miki leans down reverently and touches the tarmac. Ikuyo stands apart with a look of intense concentration on her face. She does the dance in her mind's eye. Hip drops, camel, arabesque, shimmy. It's not right. She's surer than ever she's missed a step.

Mama shuffles out the van and over to the Captain. She leans into him and mutters something in his ear. He nods delightedly and springs into action, waving his arms.

'Right you horrible lot. Zebra crossing. Now.' Taking all their phones from them, he hands them to Yoko. Then he positions Greg, Gary and Ikuyo on the zebra crossing so they occupy the same positions as the Beatles on the iconic cover. 'Gary, socks off – you're Macca. Greg, you look pretty chilled so you're George Harrison. Ikuyo, love, sorry and all that but someone's got to be Ringo and you're the shortest. And Miki, get to the front, and take yer mac off. John Lennon wouldn't have been seen dead in an anorak, and you're him.'

The Captain stands in the street and, blithely ignoring the honking of horns and irate yells of gridlocked commuters, holds up the oncoming traffic as Yoko films the re-enaction on everyone's phones. 'Sorry mate, can't you see the geezer's lost his shoes', he barracks one particularly insistent lorry driver as Miki, grinning from ear to ear, leads the line across the zebra once, twice… five times.

Once the photo-shoot is over The Captain leans back against his lamp-post and watches his charges as they loon about like a bunch of big kids, snapping each other pulling faces next to the Abbey Road sign and on the steps of the studios. Eventually, Gary, Greg and Ikuyo spot a convenience store and head for it, but Miki stays where he's so often seen himself, in his mind's eye. The drizzle has stopped so it must be the light hitting the moisture in the air that makes tiny iridescent rainbows halo around the outlines of hands and faces. Perhaps it's also the rain that causes the optical illusion of four ghostly men in familiar late '60s gear, who grin self-consciously at each other before taking their places on the zebra crossing.

The one with bare feet takes a step, utters a very human squeal and hops frantically about in a way that never made it onto the album cover.

'What you doing, divvy? Did you tread on a tin-tac, like?' The dark-suited one turns round first.

'What happened to your shoes, Paul?' says the denim-clad one in lugubrious tones.

'He asked the cobbler to fix a hole. The rain kept coming in.' The long-haired one in the white suit looks as if he couldn't care less. 'I'm sackin' off. Tara.' With that, he vanishes into thin air, leaving an iridescent Lennon-shaped hole in the ether. Miki, seeing but not believing, stretches out a trembling hand to catch the rainbow, but the illusion slips though his fingers.

The Captain and Mama raise their hands in a farewell to the departing spirits as Yoko comes up behind them, leans into the selfie frame, focuses her iPhone on the Captain and snaps.

'He flamingo.'

Gary, now with his shoes back on, and Greg both look at her quizzically. The Captain shakes his head and an Access All Areas pass falls from his hat onto the floor. 'Nah, no clue mate. Me neither.'

'Is so.' Yoko nods emphatically. 'He flamingo.'

The Captain picks up the pass where it has fallen, and instead of stowing it back in his hatband, reaches up to his hat and plucks out the handful of laminates, which he passes round with as great a solemnity as if he were handing out ritual doses of peyote.

'Guard these with care and regard these, seekers after the truth of the rock'n'roll lifestyle, as your tickets to ride. For now I will indeed provide you with access to all areas, and by that I do not mean that you will have access to the rider and the groupies, for that is only for liggers, not those who would commune with the spirit. By that I do in fact mean that we will access all areas. Ladles and jellyspoons, are you ready to take some strange trip out there?'

'Duck Butter and...' For the first time since they embarked, Greg looks impressed.

'Yeah, that's right.' For a second, a look of immense pride passes across the Captain's face, but when he clocks Greg's questioning expression, his face goes blank. 'I mean, back in the van with you. Anchors a-weigh. Mama, stop off at the garage. Feeding time at the rock'n'roll zoo.'

He re-emerges with an assortment of Ginsters, pre-packed sausage rolls, Mars Bars and packets of barbeque-flavoured nuts, which he lobs into the back of the van.

'Standard on the road nosh.' He upends a packet of dry roast peanuts into his own mouth. 'Get stuck in. Absolutely nothing of any nutritional value in any of it, which is why Mama has brought her own salad. Rock'n'roll feeds the spirit and has a horrible tendency to leave the body to fend for itself. But the road of excess can lead to the palace of wisdom. '

He points proudly to himself. 'These are lessons I learned as I journeyed through the underworld on the road to the palace of enlightenment.' The more arcane the Captain's utterances become, the more bewildered his passengers look, although speech is impossible because their mouths are clogged up with pasties, chocolate bars and peanuts.

'Got myself a bit pissed up. In a right state. Lost it for a bit. Didn't know my arse from my elbow for quite some time.'

As if through a glass darkly, we see a vision of the Captain, passed out in a grimy alley on a pile of black refuse sacks. He is surrounded by crows, which watch over him as he mutters incoherently to himself.

'Yeah, it was my journey to encounter my dark self. A necessary step in the vision quest, for those who would guide others. Makes you realise things. Understand the path you need to be on. Which is where I'm taking you. It's time for one of the most important landmarks in rock, where you can commune with the spirit, if you are so inclined. Has everyone got their passes?' Ikuyo, Miki, Yoko, Greg and Gary all wave their laminates in the air. 'Mama, next stop Camden.'

Mama pokes the cassette player again, and the tune changes to bluesy pub rock sung by a man who sounds as if he's been gargling with sand and gravel. It's such a funky trucking tune that everyone is snapping their fingers as the van sputters into life again and sets off.

'Now, I'm going to show you the most significant venue in the history of rock. The Electric Ballroom. In Camden. And I'll tell you for why it's important.' The Captain pauses dramatically. 'It's where I met Mama.'

Flashback. In a ticket queue in a scuzzy underground venue, we see two young, slim, beautiful people: a black-clad girl with long hair and a leather-jacketed young man with an unruly mane of black curls. As they gaze at each other, a heart shape forms itself around them in red neon, and pulses, increasing in intensity with each beat.

'Twenty-five years ago, and we've been inseparable ever since. No one's ever had a second thought about the band that played that night but to me and Mama they were the most important band in the world. The lesson to be learned is never duck out of the chance to see a shitty gig because you never know when it's your turn for your life to change. Rock and roll can make all your dreams come true, and mine did, that night. I met my twin soul.'

He looks lovingly at the heap of rags driving the van. Under his gaze, the woman stalls it again.

'Back into neutral babe.' She slams the gear stick back and forth. Greg looks as if he's about to fall off the mattress again, and this time Gary puts out a hand to stop him.

The van lurches forward. 'So yeah, rock and roll makes anything possible. Like us. Here we are. After all these years she still dances in a ring of fire. And I stoke her bellows. And you know what?' He looks at the woman hunkered over the steering wheel. 'Mama can't drive.'

The punters draw an appalled collective breath.

'Right.' The Captain doffs his hat at the punters. 'Onwards and upwards. Mama, take it to the bridge.'

Mama points the van towards the wall.

'That's a wall! There isn't any bridge!' scream Greg and Gary in unison.

The Captain shakes his head in disappointment.

'You haven't been listening to a word I've been saying, have you?'

Gary and Greg glance at each other, as if weighing up which of them is to step up and take a stance. Greg opens his mouth.

'We were hoping this trip would pick up, along the way, but we're sorry to say it hasn't. We do feel we've been a bit short-changed.'

Gary blushes when Greg utters the word 'we' for the second time, and pipes up.

'This is just to let you know that we won't be asking for our money back, but we will be leaving a review on Trip Advisor so that other people won't make the same mistake as us.'

The Captain lowers his head, and eyeballs Greg and Gary like a bull preparing to charge.

'You don't get it, do you? You have to give it everything. No reservations. I offer you access all areas. Of course it's ridiculous. I'm ridiculous. You're ridiculous. Rock'n'roll is ridiculous... but therein lies its beauty. Have faith, my friend. I believe in it so much I gave it everything I had. My heart, my soul, my health, my sanity... My hair. I had lovely hair, back in the day.'

Momentarily distracted, he puts a hand to where his hair used to be, then remembers himself. 'You may think I'm a clown, but going after my rock'n'roll dream I went into the underworld. I was buried alive. I nearly lost my mind. I nearly lost everything, except the love of the woman driving this van taking you load, of, of... day trippers' – he spits the words – 'and I'm still here, still on the road, still keeping the faith, taking you on a, on a... day trip... because I still believe with my whole heart and soul. And so does Mama. And if you believe, rock'n'roll makes anything possible. It can change your lives. Make your dreams come true. Look at us. All you've got to do is open your eyes and let the world in.'

Ignoring bewildered stares from Greg and Gary, he pokes the cassette player and the first chugging bars of Golden Earring's Radar Love slam through the airwaves. The Captain cranks up the volume until it reaches its optimum point, then yells over the deafening racket. 'Mama, step on the gas, if you'd be so kind. Straight on through to the other side.'

And with that, Mama puts her foot down.

The van picks up speed. Gary grabs Greg. Ikuyo grabs Yoko and the drum case holding her topples backwards off the mattress

The van hurtles towards the wall. Greg, Gary, Miki and Ikuyo screw their eyes shut and fold themselves into the brace position.

'Hold on tight for the ride of your lives!' yowls the Captain, voice in full throttle. And as the van's occupants turn to look at him, they see him in the electrifying magnificence of his glory days, clad in skin-tight black leather, clutching the mic with his head, topped with a luxuriant mane of black curls, flung back. As fireworks explode and guitars grind out an insistent riff, we see he's commanding an audience of several thousand, waving their hands towards him in adoration.

Yoko jumps up and down in excitement. 'He flamingo,' she squeaks. 'He so flamingo!'

Mama puts her foot to the floor. All five punters squeal as if the devils and demons of whichever hell they believed in were poking them with flaming pitchforks.

'Let's go!!!!" yells the Captain.

Guitars screech and wail. The bass line is so intense it makes everyone's kidneys wobble. Drums rattle out a military crescendo. Lights flash, the world spins on its axis and the van… slams though the wall.

And carries on, picking up speed, faster and faster, as it travels onwards.

Onwards and upwards. The path feels smooth beneath the wheels. Slowly, carefully, unfolding themselves as carefully as Christmas baubles from tissue paper, the van's inhabitants look up, and then up a bit further. They are met by the sight of the Captain's beaming face, and beyond him, past the windscreen, the strangest and most beautiful road they have ever seen.

Mama is driving the van up the arc of a giant rainbow.

Moments pass in which the van's inhabitants are rapt in total silence as they contemplate the unearthly euphoria of the ride they're on. Eventually, the silence is broken by the gentle strumming of a guitar. It's the Captain, playing the chords of Woodstock with understated delicacy.

He sings, in a tender velvet croon, about being starlight and golden. He has a beautiful voice. Mama looks at him and the pupils of her eyes turn to vast, pulsating love hearts. In the same moment, Greg and Gary look at each other. Each stretches out both hands.

Gary speaks first. 'I don't mind where our baby comes from.'

Greg wipes a tear from his eye. 'I wanted it to look like you. So we look like a family.'

'We will look like a family. We'll look like our family.' Gary pulls Greg into his arms and the two men look through the tears in each other's eyes to find there's a rainbow reflected in each one.

Miki can't believe what the rainbow road is leading him to. It's the set of All You Need is Love. The Fab Four, in their finest Carnaby Street regalia, are surrounded by banks of flowers, placards with slogans, massed banks of balloons. And, sitting at John Lennon's feet amidst the beautiful people in the studio, there he is. Miki. Crossed-legged, blissed out, dressed in a military jacket with brass buttons, swaying, higher than the sun with a flower in his hair. And as he watches, John Lennon looks straight at him – him! – and sings. Passing the torch. 'Love. It is all you need,' whispers Miki. 'Yeah, yeah. Yeah.'

Yoko is scanning the view with her iPhone when a giant bird in a top hat comes into view. 'He flamingo' she shrieks, and tries to capture him, but he caws in her face and flaps away, leaving a trail of Access All Areas passes scattered on the rainbow road.

Ikuyo gazes out of the window. All she can see is the road ahead, and as far as she's concerned, it's just leading her back to the hotel, and then they'll go out to dinner, then to bed, and then it will be tomorrow and then the rest of her life, and there will barely be time for her to keep up with everything she has to do. At least gazing out of this window is peaceful... and then she catches sight of… herself, dancing with the troupe, each one in a costume sequinned in different candy colours. Red, orange, yellow, green, blue, indigo and violet. All the colours of the… She remembers all the steps. She is in violet, graceful and lovely, and above all, she has not embarrassed herself, or let the rest of the troupe down. She isn't a mother, or a wife, or a daughter or a sister or an office worker, she is just herself, dancing with her girls, and as relief floods her, she realises that there can be enough room in her world for her to make her dream come true. Without taking her hands off the wheel, Mama turns round and looks straight at her. 'If you forget the steps, just keep smiling and pick up the next beat. No-one will ever know.' Ikuyo bows from the waist and smiles and smiles. 'Thank you. Thank you.' 'That smile,' says Mama. 'They'll love you.'

The van rattles its way along the rainbow road. Peace reigns amongst its passengers, each immersed in their own thoughts, their wonderstruck expressions are those of pilgrims in the aftermath of a miraculous experience.

As the van pulls up, the Captain finishes his song, puts his guitar down and stretches.

'Job done, don't you reckon? Beautiful dreams purveyed to those whose worlds have become too small for them, satisfaction guaranteed. Come on babe, we've got a garden to get back to. Cats to feed.'

He cranks the van door open and pitches himself headlong through it, catching his boot in the footwell, and landing, sprawling, on the gravel surface of… the car park in Vauxhall where the Rock'n'Roll Dream Tour set out from only hours before.

He picks himself up, dusts himself down and swaggers to the back, with a flourish, he opens the door. The passengers, wobbly on unsteady legs, hold onto each other as they clamber out. Once out, they stand around the Captain in an awestruck circle.

'We are so…' sighs Miki.

'So…' sighs Greg.

'So,' sighs Gary.

'Thankful,' manages Ikuyo.

'Wow,' exhales Miki. 'Wow.'

Everyone nods in agreement. The circle closes in a little tighter round the Captain. They do not want to let him go. He rocks on the soles of his feet but they've got him surrounded. Eventually, he puts up a hand.

'Well, right, show's over. Ladies and gentlemen, it's been a pleasure.'

'Encore.' Miki knows his rock'n'roll etiquette. 'You give us encore.'

The others take up the chant and stand round the Captain, stamping and clapping. 'Encore. Encore.'

The Captain shrugs modestly, but it's obvious he's pleased. Mama appears next to him, proffering his guitar. 'Give them one of yours.'

He nods, shuffles, clears his throat, and essays a quick strum before looking up. 'This one's called Forest Dancer,' he offers. 'I wrote it for Mama.'

He starts, softly, to sing complicated words against a lilting lullaby of a tune, which mounts in intensity

until the Captain beckons Mama with a finger. His voice rising, he sings the words 'spinning, spinning,' over and over, and as his voice rises in intensity, Mama starts to dance, spinning round and round, faster and faster, until her swirling blur of skirts floats up from the ground and, pulling the Captain into her orbit, lifts off into the sky.

Greg, Gary, Ikuyo and Miki watch as the Captain and Mama whirl upwards, hand in hand, moving faster and faster, higher and higher. With Yoko filming everything on her iPhone, we see them rise up into the clouds, until they turn into a tiny, heart-shaped speck, and then vanish.

Yoko points the iPhone at herself and pulls a cute selfie face. 'He so flamingo', she tells the camera. Back in the hotel, she will spend time with the Garageband and iMovie apps on her phone and by evening, she will upload the clip onto YouTube. She's captured everything – the crossing at Abbey Road, the moment the van slammed through the wall, the rainbow road, the crow, flying past in his topper, and the Captain and Mama, making their unforgettable exit. She creates a soundtrack – a haunting, minimalist tune she calls Yoko's Number One Dream. And right at the end, whilst Yoko is doing her selfie-face sign off, if you look very closely, you might notice a crow, in the far background, picking up an Access All Areas pass from the floor by where the van was parked and tucking it under its wing. Because social media is second nature to

Yoko, by the end of the week the clip will have gone viral, amassing more than a million hits.

It's still doing the rounds, cropping up on people's Facebook feeds in discussions about the Rock'n'Roll Dream Tour. Inspired seekers still make their way to the car park in Vauxhall, in greater numbers than ever, but they wait in vain, because since the day they took to the sky, the Captain and Mama have never yet put in an appearance. The seekers still come though, and hang about, restlessly vaping and peering at the road at every white van that passes. It's become an act of faith to imagine that one day, if they all believe hard enough, one of them will be the Rock'n'Roll Dream Tour bus, ready to take another load of passengers on the ride of a lifetime.

GOOD JOURNEY

Once upon a long time ago, in a record shop near Leicester Square, Lula opened her large black patent handbag in front of a man she knew from her record collection.

He made music that contained all the stories that had captured her imagination when she was small. On his lapel he wore a brooch covered in gemstones, but his eyes twinkled brighter than its jewels with the kindness that comes from seeing further than the surface of things. We shall call him the Alchemist, because that's how Lula thought of him.

'That looks like Mary Poppins' handbag,' he remarked. 'I wish I could do magic out of it like she did,' huffed Lula, who couldn't find her purse. 'I expect you can, if you try,' smiled the Alchemist. Then he paid for his Massive Attack CDs and went on his way, his ragged red velvet coat swirling round his ankles.

Lula was filled with an intense yearning to follow the Alchemist out of Tower Records and go with him into the forest where she felt sure he belonged. Instead, she got the train home.

Because she had read so many fairy tales, Lula had always known that there was more to life than meets the eye. Still, she was disappointed that it tended to obey the laws of realism rather than those of magic. Her godmother gave her gift sets from Marks &

Spencer, rather than three wishes. She kissed a load of frogs and not one of them had the decency to turn into a prince. She never met an animal that gave her good advice in human language when she found herself getting into difficulties, and whenever she told a lie, her nose remained resolutely the same size. The big black patent bag was useful for carrying books and iPhones and chocolate truffles and cosmetics and a Bag for Life, but that was about it.

Lula had a realistic turn of mind, and she got on with what her existence offered, appreciating its small joys and trying not to be upset when it didn't live up to the version she created in her imagination. She had a job she liked, and friends who were pleased to see her. Her flat was nice, and she earned enough money not to have to worry about paying the bills. Gradually, she stopped buying books, and just read the news online. But over the years, whenever she thought about it, she always regretted that she had gone back to Chiswick the day she met the Alchemist.

Much later, she met the Storyteller. His mother had taken Thalidomide before he was born. It hadn't had an effect on his body, but the stories that fell out of his brain were strange, misshapen things, with a sad and beautiful logic beneath the twisted humour.

The Storyteller was gentle and clever and troubled, and very dear to Lula. He lived in a world of his own and they met, mostly, in cyberspace. He emailed her stories, which she read before going to bed. They didn't have happy endings, and they filtered into her dreams, so that her sleeping life was more eventful than her waking one. Lula accepted that this was the way things were, but it got on her nerves sometimes. She realised she wanted the stories in her life, not in her mind. She wondered if that was all there was for her, and the longer it went on, the sadder it made her feel.

One day at work, her friend Vick, who understood that laughter was the best medicine when people were unhappy, took Lula in hand. 'You need to go dancing. You're always saying there isn't enough dancing. And I know just the thing,' she said. Then Vick made a few phone calls that put them both on the guest list for the gypsy punk band that were playing in town that night.

It was more carnival than concert: a motley crew cavorting dementedly to the most insistent rhythms Lula had ever heard. She was transported, dancing uncontrollably to music that made her blood cells pulsate and her feet feel as if they were alight, unable to peel her eyes from the spectacle in front of her.

The Singer had a ringmaster's moustache and swivelling green eyes that glowed like absinthe as he walked from the stage onto the extended hands of the audience. A woman took off the enormous drum she was playing and balanced it on the crowd so she could clamber onto it and carry on battering seven devils from its skin. The Violinist fiddled with such demonic speed that his bow burst into flames as he played. Smoke billowed around him in great clouds, so that Lula could not tell where it ended and the wispy tails of his long grey hair began.

When it ended, Lula was covered in sweat and grinning from ear to ear. 'Come on,' urged Vick. 'Let's go thank them.' 'No,' said Lula, unable to think of any words that would express how she felt. 'I'll stay here.' But Vick had hold of her hand, and was dragging her across the floor to where the Violinist was packing snakes of electric cable into a box. He kissed Vick's hand with old-fashioned courtesy as she told him how much she'd enjoyed the show. Then it was Lula's turn.

'Thank you,' she stammered. As he brought her hand to his lips, she raised her eyes to look at him. He didn't let go of her fingers, and looked into her face with an intensity that sent an electric shock through her. His eyes were jet black in his swarthy pirate's face, glinting with the promise of secrets waiting to be revealed. As he looked into her, Lula was reminded of the Alchemist, and how she had turned away from what she had most wanted.

'Vick,' she muttered as they staggered back to their coats. 'I'm not coming to work tomorrow. I know it sounds silly, and I'll probably regret it. But I'm running away to join the circus.'

Vick put her arms round Lula and told her that if that was what she wanted, then that was what she ought to do. 'It's time you stopped being sensible,' she said affectionately. 'Go. Follow your dreams.'

'I'll miss the Storyteller,' whispered Lula.

'You can't miss someone who was never really there,' said Vick. 'It's all imagination with him. Go get some stories of your own.'

'I'll miss you, too,' said Lula sadly.

'Yes, but I'm real,' replied Vick. 'If the grass isn't greener where you're going, you can come home again. I'll be there when you get back.'

Lula had tears in her eyes as she hugged Vick in parting and made her way to the stage door. She fished in her bag, rolled a cigarette and lit it, and wondered what on earth she was doing. Part of her wanted to start wearing purple, but another bit wondered if there was enough in her purse for a taxi.

Finally, bedraggled and tattered, the band began to emerge into the chilly March night. The Singer had a striped towel wrapped around his shoulders and the ends of his moustache quivered of their own accord as they registered the freezing temperature. The woman with the drum hugged it to her as if it were an animal, stroking it to make up for having hit it so hard. The Violinist carried his fiddle close to his chest, but when he spotted Lula, he tucked it under his chin and, very softly, began to play a gentle, lilting melody. He looked once in her direction and tilted his chin as if to say, come with us, and given permission by the music that drew her in, she fell into their ranks as they processed across the town.

Eventually they reached a brightly painted caravan and, one after another, clambered inside. Lula didn't

think there would be room for the entire troupe in such a small space, but they arranged themselves round the samovar at the caravan's centre, and the Singer made a place for Lula by clearing a pile of socks and pants out of an accordion case so that she could sit in it.

The woman with the drum stashed it by clipping it to the ceiling. The samovar was lit, and tea made which was served in small glasses with a slice of lemon. Bottles of cherry and honey vodka were produced from instrument cases and passed around. The Singer began to sing in a language Lula didn't understand, and the drummer beat a rhythm on his knees and on the wooden box that was his seat. The Violinist caressed his instrument, drawing the bow tenderly across the strings, coaxing strains of sound from it that filled the caravan with music that told tales of mountains and camp fires and men who flashed their eyes at black-haired women. These figures danced out of the shadows and filled Lula's head until she fell asleep, curled up in the accordion case, overcome with excitement, emotion and vodka.

She woke in the middle of the night, cramped and concertina-ed in her case. Emerging awkwardly from it, she saw the figure of the Violinist stretched out on the bench beside her, his fiddle clasped tenderly to the broad barrel of his chest. With the utmost care, she removed it from his fingers and laid it gently in her big black patent bag. Then she tucked herself in its place under the Violinist's chin. She didn't sleep, because she didn't need to dream. She had begun to live in a story, and this was only just the beginning. Lula smiled to herself in the darkness as she wondered where the road would take her.

TEMPTATION

There is a devil that sometimes dances outside Waitrose. In repose he slumps in a red heap of broken body parts topped off with a grinning, peeling mask. A Mister Punch gone to the bad, or worst. His dance is a jerky jig without any jollity – a purposefully horrible choreography that brings to mind mechanical Morris dancers.

It's even more unpleasant when he speaks. I hear the screeching of crows and jackals, accompanied by a jangling, discordant whine, and feel a sub-bass rumbling that rattles my liver into a queasy commotion. I can easily make him out over the racket though.

'*Salted caramels,*' he snickered yesterday. '*Rose and violet creams. Gravadlax.*'

I'm only too suggestible to temptation, and he's in a good spot to catch me at moments of weakness.

He gets me each time. He always knows what it is I really want. I was telling myself I'd go to Cath Kidston but the frocks I can't get into depress me. The devil knows what guilty secrets I've got stashed in my shopper. I'd call them dirty pleasures but high-end groceries are my particular sin. At least it's venal, not cardinal.

Yesterday, I called my assistant into my office. 'Stellar, why did you send this out?' I pointed to the line on the press release where she'd written: 'I would just like to be a poo and say that we can't organise festival tickets.'

Stellar looked at the newly tattooed owl on her hand and shrugged. 'Well cos they all think I will and I just can't.'

I gave up. Because, as that dreadful advert says, I'm worth it. There is a large gap between what I thought my life would be, and what it actually is. That's where the devil gets in. I can see him hoofing his way through his grim soft-shoe shuffle as I'm reading Stellar's inanities. Worse, through the crows cackling and the jackals howling and the sick-making shudder of the sub-bass, and newly, this time, the scratting of rat claws, I can clearly hear him taunting me.

'Wasabi peas. Spanakopita. Marinaded chilli olives. Plum clafoutis.'

I eat them all at home, where there's no-one to look. I feel sick afterwards, but even that's part of the pleasure.

It's not that I haven't dieted. I've tried most of them, existing in the wilderness between chicken breasts and fillets of steamed white fish – no butter – by trying not to think about food. Now there's a laugh. All anorexics think about is food. All bulimics think about, is food. And those nuns who starved themselves to get closer to their heavenly bridegroom? The way I see it fasting doesn't make you think about God. It just makes you think about food.

I haven't always thought about food. I used to be hungry for success, chasing the next big slice of the public relations pie. I was hot sauce in music PR. All the big names, all the headliners. Now even I've barely heard of my acts, let alone the public, or at least anyone old enough to drink legally in pubs. And anyone would be struck with a sense of existential emptiness and driven to gourmet snacks if they had to spend their working mornings awaiting Stellar's regular Friday lol-cat press release.

Whatever she's meant to be publicising, she does it by the simple expedient of emailing pictures of what she calls smol kittehs, and promising to send out product to anyone who asks.

'Well it works. I get peeps to see my bands. Peeps likes kittehs,' Stellar argues when I pull her up about it.

Perhaps she's got a point. Perhaps I'm too old to be doing this. I nearly passed up the last client I took on because his hairstyle looked like an old lady's feather hat that had started to moult. Flicky tufts sticking out at all angles. Stellar got national reviews for his first gigs.

When I stumped past Waitrose after the last lol-cat mail, the devil caught my eye. '*Cardamom shortbread*,' he huffed, the steam coming out of his nostrils indicating that he was out of breath after a diabolically determined hornpipe.

'Tapenade. Quail's eggs. And a tin of Spam, because even ironic food can be forbidden fruit.'

He was marking time, and I fell into step beside him. One-two, one-two. It's a long time since I had a dance. He looked at me approvingly, and turned to me with a broken-tooth grin that showed the serrated edges of his saw-edge molars. His sulphur breath sent me reeling and the concrete floor turned into the wet barnacled wood of a ship tossing in a storm as the seas came up to meet me. The devil caught me before I went crashing to the pavement and bent me backwards into a tango lunge.

'And when you've eaten it all, what then?'

The devil's eyes boiled black and the sound of baying wolverines echoed through the precinct as he swept me up and into the air, and then hung me, suspended on strings as if I were some giant puppet, directly over the spot where I had so nearly fainted.

'When you've eaten it all, and eaten it all again, and eaten it all some more, your insides will still gnaw with hunger. There isn't enough food in the world to satisfy the hollow inside you.'

The devil extended his red right hand towards the horizon. Fingernails charred as if they had been held in the fire sent sparks into the middle distance, and suddenly I realised that all the houses and offices below, and all the people, and birds and animals, were not made of flesh and blood, but of bread and wine; cake and pie; delicate pasty and exquisite liqueurs.

The devil jerked on the strings that held my shoulders and back, lurching me forward so that I was horizontal.

'Look down. Everything beneath you could be inside you. Will you still settle for a sneaky tin of Spam when all this could be yours, bite after bite, any flavour you want, to consume at your pleasure?'

Oh, my mouth watered. To gorge at my leisure on anything that took my fancy. Dinner plates passed before my eyes, each laden with the feast of a lifetime.

But working in PR has taught me one valuable lesson. There's no such thing as a free lunch.

'What is it that you want in return?' I asked the devil.

'Oh, not your soul. That's... immaterial. But you're a professional. You're not at the top of your game anymore but you were good. I thought you could reinvent me for a new generation. Give me a make-over. Make me TV-friendly. Look at me. I've got the skills. I used to be A-list. I've got loads of back catalogue. I could do a comeback tour. You could get me on that X-Factor. I'd wing it. '

To prove his point, the devil unfurled a set of leathery pinions and flapped them, filling the air with a rattling clatter, a whooshing of fetid air, and showers of dust and grit.

'Now look at you. Career going down the toilet. New generation coming up behind you. We're both

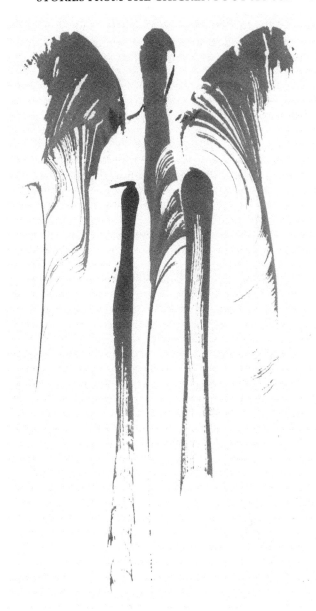

hungry for change. You can't tell me you don't miss the big time. We could do each other a favour.'

The devil pulled me upright so that my legs were in the usual place, pointing downwards, then jerked the strings.

And that did it for me. After all those years of putting up with tantrums from no-mark egotists. Pouting prima donnas. Demanding divas. Self-obsessed flakes. People who thought they had the right to dominion.

This was the final straw.

I looked the devil in the eye. Sharks swam in the murky blackness of his pupils, and leviathans called from the depths, but I held his gaze.

'Not going to happen.'

And with that, the heavens cracked and the sun turned black and red the moon. And the devil's fingers turned to giant scissors, and he chopped the strings.

I came to on the pavement to find an old lady helping me to my feet.

'I think you fell on your pistachio creams, dear. Can you stand up?' She held out a hand whose papery skin was scented with lavender. I wasn't tempted to take even the tiniest nibble. And the only sounds I could hear were the noises of ordinary people going about their daily business. Buying groceries. Eating snacks.

I made it back to the office and sent everyone home. I stayed there and went online, then called a liquidator.

Then I went home, ate cheese on toast, and watched Masterchef on catch-up. I knew what I was going to do.

It was time for a career change. A lifestyle change. It was time I opened a new business. A chi-chi little boutique. Selling cup cakes so pretty no-one would resist.

As the devil said, I've got the skills.

Without any help from the devil, or anyone else for that matter, I was going to have my cake. And eat it, too.

I DREAM OF JEAN GENIE

The gig, for once, was a blinder. The crowd surfed, the pit moshed and the band staggered backstage on bandy legs like pirates.

'Where did that come from? I mean, we're The Hopeless. Traditionally, the rubbish support act.' Nathan the bass player was the sarcastic one.

'That's what happens when you wish for something hard enough. It's time we had our break. I mean, we should be famous!' Corey, the singer, thought he was entitled to behave like a rock star.

Jed nodded. No-one could see his face behind his hair. He was the lead guitarist. He didn't say anything. He never said anything.

Paul the drummer was the practical one. Sitting at the back behind his kit, he noticed things. 'It was Jeanie. The belly dancer. When she made her entrance. That's when it happened.'

The pocket redhead in the spangled gauze two-piece had turned up right on cue for their grunge cover of *The Jean Genie*. When Corey howled 'Let yourself go!' she'd made her entrance, whirling so fast that sparks flew from her to all corners of the grimy Old Street backroom. And then she jumped up with sure, slender feet onto Paul's cymbals and shivered and quivered until the silvery shimmering sound of the oscillating metal sent the crowd into a collective ecstasy and they all threw their hands in

the air, and didn't notice that the flying sparks had burned holes in the sticky pub carpet.

'It was the music. They were digging the music. And me. Getting a vibe off me.' Corey could never stand it when it wasn't about him. 'She was just stage decoration. I ordered her specially.'

'Does she do private dances?' Nathan had nearly tripped over his lead when she sashayed over to his part of the stage.

'Hey, don't talk about Jeanie like that. She can hear you. She's over there.' Paul had been brought up in a council flat in Stepney where manners were important.

They all turned to where Paul was pointing. There she was, perched with perfect poise in her Turkish trouser suit on top of an amp.

'Where did you come from?'

'I got her from an agency. It's no big deal.' Corey got brattish when he wasn't the centre of attention. 'I picked this one because she looked kind of retro, like the actress in *I Dream of Jeannie*. But there are all sorts. You click on a lamp when you find one you like. You can get your rocks off over them online later, loser-boy. Fat ones. Thin ones.'

'Ones with ginger hair.' They all jumped. The dancer had a note of steel to her beautifully modulated voice. Something about her made you want to stand up straight.

'Slave girls, sold here, fifty bob a lump.' Paul remembered his old nana singing that. A comedy song. Music hall. Something about an old bazaar in Cairo.

'And something for your Aunty Fanny. That's the one. Not a lot of people know it. I've come from Portobello Road, and by the way, my name isn't Jeanie. That's only for the website. It's Isabella. But I am a genie, and before I go off in a puff of smoke, which by the way can't come soon enough, you have two wishes left. You get three and he' – she pointed rather scornfully at Corey – 'has already used up one of them on making a raging success of this pub gig. That no-one will remember, because the Hackney haircuts out there are all off their faces.'

As a man, the band stood up and looked accusingly at Corey. Lost for words in the face of Isabella's tirade, he sat with his mouth open like a fish.

Isabella saved him from his struggle to find something to say. 'Look at you all, slouching!' She sounded like a schoolmarm. 'Your posture is terrible! You need to stand up straight and open your chests. Yoga, that's what you need.'

Paul felt himself involuntarily stretching out. It felt good. He tried it a bit more and was pleased with the results.

A low groan sounded beneath Jed's overhanding hair. 'Dude, we're a grunge band! Doing that would change the way we play! I wish we could stay the same for ever.'

It was the first thing the band had ever heard him say.

Isabella raised her eyebrows. 'To coin a cliché, your wish is my...'

'Hold up!' Paul suddenly felt six inches taller, and as if what he had to say was terribly important.

Ignoring the rest of the band, he looked directly at Isabella. 'I'd like to live happily ever after.'

Isabella glanced at Jed, Corey and Nathan. 'Command,' she uttered dismissively. Then she looked at Paul. A faint smile crossed her lips.

'You'll have to do yoga,' she said.

There was a puff of smoke, and she vanished.

The venue turned Corey, Jed and Nathan, who had been frozen in time ever since Isabella said the word 'command', into a backstage installation. At first it was an in-crowd secret but then *Metro* got hold of the story and ran it as a double-page spread. After that The Hopeless was on the top ten lists of visitor attractions for the kind of tourist who booked accommodation through Airbnb and liked eating in independent cafes specialising in varieties of cereal.

Paul knows that wishes really do come true. He lives for six months each year in Kerala, where Isabella holds yoga retreats, and the other six months in the attic flat over her studio off the Portobello Road. He switched from a full drum kit to playing hand percussion, and is in demand in his own right as a session musician, and as a belly dance accompanist for Isabella – they've even devised a routine where she performs an entire number balanced on top of one darabuka whilst he plays another. On their nights off, they sing along to old music hall tunes on YouTube.

RATS IN THE KITCHEN

Masha was a classic case of the Valium housewife in spite of not being married and never having had psychiatric treatment. At twenty-five, her daily routine was get up, take drugs, go to work, come home, take drugs, sit on the sofa, take drugs, fall into bed. Her drugs were off-prescription; she self-medicated. It didn't really matter what they were; she had what you might call a psychological dependency rather than anything physical.

Sometimes she had sex with Joe, her boyfriend, but more often than not she tried to get away without having to do it. Sometimes, instead of going to work, she sat for hours, wired and scared, pinned to her seat on the Circle Line, going round and round without getting off. Sometimes, when she got home before Joe did, she'd sit in the dark in the bedroom, rocking backwards and forwards. Sometimes, he found her there. 'What on earth are you doing?' he'd ask, and she wouldn't be able to tell him she'd been trying to will him not to come home. Joe met Masha when she lived in happy nightlife squalor. He wanted her because he thought she made him look more interesting than he was. He loved the time he walked into his office and proudly informed his colleagues that he'd been at an illegal after-club drinking den with her, where he'd drunk home-made poteen and smoked sensi and then come straight into work without going to sleep at all. The admiring looks on their faces had made him feel cool. When he took her to the pub to meet his workmates, her multi-coloured hair and ambivalent smile excited a degree of sexual speculation amongst his colleagues that he felt reflected enormously well upon him.

After a prolonged siege which included roses, presents, weekends away, lots of giggling and continuously enthusiastic sex, he'd convinced her that she wanted to pack up her belongings into a shopping trolley and her cat into a cat-basket and come to live in a happy-ever-after egg box with him. The timing was good; she hadn't had a proper boyfriend for over a year, she owned masses of back-rent and her flatmate had taken to painting everything in the flat black. But once she'd moved in, Joe didn't want her to be interesting any more. When she was, he felt he wasn't the centre of her world. He liked doing coupley things like the shopping, together, and having friends round (his). He wanted her to spend a lot of time with his mother. He disapproved of her old ways, which had initially seemed lively and appealing, and every now and then, when she sneaked off with a friend to revisit her old life, he was a bit sniffy about it. He felt there was something about her he'd never quite managed to catch and tame, which made her seem unknowably remote at times, as if she was miles away even when she was laying next to him in the bed.

Joe was the kind of man who always brought flowers and chocolates home on a Friday, on his way home from his well-paid job with good career prospects. He'd never have admitted it even to himself, but he liked it best when she was ill, so he could look after her. Tucked up on the sofa in their rented living room, she seemed frail and vulnerable rather than distanced and otherworldly. 'You're so sweet,' he'd gush, bringing her flowers and herbal remedies. The flowers stayed in their vases until all the petals dropped off and she put the herbal remedies down the sink when Joe wasn't looking.

She'd also medicine herself when he wasn't looking, and gradually the colour began to drain out of her. When the washing machine broke down, sending a torrent of soapy water gushing all over the lino in the bathroom, she phoned him at the office. 'The washing machine's broken down,' she squawked. 'You've got to come home and mend it. I don't know what to do.' He did come home, leaving unfinished work on his desk, and he did mend it, and afterwards he felt very pleased with himself. 'Poor silly little thing,' he thought tenderly. 'She'd fall apart if I wasn't there.'

Masha seemed to spend a lot of time in the kitchen. Joe liked to be well catered for. If he didn't feel his stomach was pampered, he didn't feel loved. Masha got hooked on the soothing rhythms of cutting up and weighing and watching things not burning. Her brain could detach itself from any emotional engagement with what she was doing whilst nevertheless being assured of a result. She felt like a human kitchen device, a stirrer, chopper, blender. Some kind of human Magimix. She'd watch herself as if from down a very long tunnel, a tiny figure moving according to a set of preplanned steps.

Joe wasn't allowed in the kitchen. She liked it that there was a part of the flat he didn't fill. When he hung around, hovering in the doorway, it made her impatient, and on bad days, panic stricken, as if she was under attack. 'Get out!' she'd squawk, backing herself into a corner. 'Let me get on with it! I can't bear it when you hover!' At those times, Joe would console himself with the thought of PMT and make himself behave with extra tolerance.

Sometimes, Joe would go to conferences, which meant he'd be away from home for a few days, or even the odd week. When this happened, Masha would phone in sick and sit on the sofa with the cat, gazing into space, which, free from the invader, was all hers. It was on a morning like this, eyes glazed contentedly over and a mug of coffee in her hand, that she realised they had rats. Just beyond the living room at the far end of the corridor by the open back door, she could see an enormous rodent helping itself out of the cat's bowl. It took her several transfixed moments to work out that it was real.

It was so large and mangy it made her flesh crawl. At the sight of its beady eyes, scrofulous coat and scaly whiplash tail, Masha came back to herself with a jolt. She gazed in horror as it bolted the cat's dinner and oozed its way under the inch-high gap under the bathroom door. She watched paralysed as the cat jumped off the sofa and scurried behind it. Then Masha seized her mobile, jumped onto the nearest table and telephoned the one person she knew could deal with it.

'Mother!' she shrieked. 'An enormous rat has just vanished into the lavatory!' Her mother, despite the bad tidings, was delighted to hear Masha sounding with it. 'Go and put on your biggest boots,' she said sensibly, 'and find a big stick.' Masha did what she was told, but before she could attack the rat, it slithered out from its hiding place and, rudely helping itself from the cat's bowl again, scurried out of the back door. 'And you're no use,' she hissed exasperatedly at the cat, who gazed back at her inscrutably.

Masha sat back on the sofa. She hadn't used her brain for so long that it felt odd, but gradually some facts filtered through. London was in the grip of its worst-ever rodent infestation. You were never more than two yards away from a rat. Sundry recent patterings and scufflings and bitten bin-bags, which Masha had put down to the cat doing her nocturnal thing suddenly, took on sinister overtones.

Every time anything in the house creaked, Masha imagined it was caused by the army of rats, on the move. Rats outnumbered the city's human inhabitants by millions. And the rats themselves were mutating, breeding themselves into ever larger, stronger and more poison-resistant species. It was called survival of the fittest, and all the rats were in prime fighting condition.

She remembered hazily how a friend's derelict flat had been infested by rats who'd eaten through the brickwork, developed an immunity to Warfarin, invited all their rat-friends round to share the feast of poison which had been left for them, smacked their lips over the delicacy and come back for more. Masha recalled how urban myth had it that the rats travelled on the underground, the scourge of the Metropolitan line, looking for places where there were good chances of finding a bolt-hole to house their ever-increasing numbers. Her friend had moved out, at first temporarily, and then for good. The rats had won. Now it was Masha's turn. The cat took off with her tail in the air, at a jaunty angle, which seemed to suggest she washed her paws of the whole thing. She miaowed gently but firmly as Masha tried to call her back, as if to say that she was sorry. Masha was on her own.

That night, preternaturally aware of anything that suggested rodents, she realised she had a full-scale occupation on her hands. Her eyes were out on stalks as a rat watched Netflix with her, settled into the shade behind Joe's precious X-box. Gnawed holes in the bin liners she'd left outside convinced her that the rats were helping themselves to leftovers she'd scraped into the rubbish. She caught a glimpse of a rat preening itself in the bathroom mirror. A brave, solitary rat made its way along the corridor to

join her in her bedroom. When she heard scrapings and scufflings, her initial thought was that it was a rustling paper bag. When she realised it was alive and doing the rat dance of the boudoir, she hid under the covers and wished desperately that she had a something to batter it with. She didn't dare get out of bed to find a weapon, so she stayed where she was and quivered.

She hardly slept. When she got up, the rats, overnight, had made their presence felt. The day before, they'd been inconspicuous, vanishing when they heard the tread of Masha's footstep. But once in occupation, they got cocky. One fronted her out in the bathroom, staring insolently at her as if to say, why should I go just because you're here? Masha screamed and shouted and stamped, and eventually the rat disappeared down a hole with an insolent flick of its tail, as if it was doing her a favour. Masha couldn't help feeling it had given her the rodent equivalent of a finger. It set off a reaction she hadn't expected: she felt more alive, more energised, than she had for a year.

It was ages since she'd done anything without consulting Joe, but she felt a new sense of determination. She went online, and looked up pest control. They promised to send someone round the same afternoon. Masha dug out the poker and sat on the sofa. She'd forgotten to take any drugs all day. Instead, she poured herself a stiff vodka. As she slugged it back, she silently vowed a toast to revenge

As promised, the rat man made his entrance. He was unexpectedly prompt, and not at all what Masha had envisaged. When her friend had had rats, the pest controller sent to deal with them had been rodent-like himself, with hairy, pouchy cheeks, beady eyes, elongated front teeth and furtive, jerky, shuffling movements. It had crossed Masha's mind that he might have been on the side of the rats because none of the rodents had actually died as a result of the poison he'd left. Conspiracy theories had riddled her mind for ages after that; they were one of the things she'd dwelt on obsessively whilst riding round and round on the Circle line.

Fey and fairy-like, Masha's rat-man couldn't have been more different. This was no ordinary little man carrying a bucket of poison. He was slim, lithe and dark. You could have eaten your dinner off his cheekbones. He had a sly foreign accent. He looked like a pixie. Masha stared at him for a moment before she noticed what he was wearing. Rats' tails and paws dripped from his belt, decorated his shirt and encircled his hat. A necklace of rat's bones was knotted around his neck and a polished, shining rat's skull was pinned to the lapel of his jacket as a brooch. Masha's jaw dropped.

The rat-man looked understanding. 'You see I am wearing some rat things,' he said in broken English, which revealed a broken tooth at the front of his mouth. 'I am born in the Year of the Rat. I live with rats. I understand rats. To fight them I have to know their ways.'

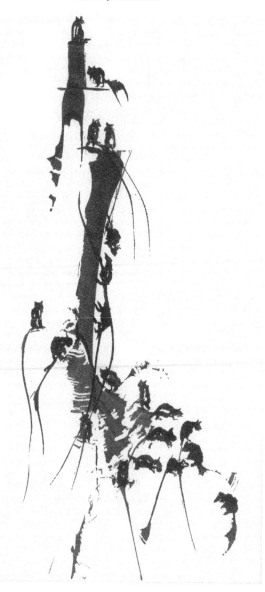

Masha's jaw was still on her chest. She shook her head uncomprehendingly. The rat-man smiled. His broken tooth flashed at her disarmingly. Masha felt herself staring, then beckoned him inside.

'To be a person who can make rats go away, I have to be like them. I have to understand what it feels like to be a rat,' he explained, leaning comfortably against the kitchen door. Masha put the kettle on. She still hadn't said anything except to ask him if he'd like a drink. 'So to make me a little of a rat myself, I wear rat things. I try to think my way into what it feels like in that skin. Looking always for an opportunity, or a place, to find a way in. To be always hated and to have not to care, just to make a place for myself. To be the thing that is disgusting, just for doing what it cannot help. So maybe, by wearing their flesh and their bones, I show them that I do not hate them, even that I respect them. Because everything that lives has some purpose. But also it is my job to make the rats not be where they are not wanted. I have to make them go away. Go to someplace else.'

Masha would never have imagined that anyone could be mystical about working as a pest controller. Now she had a rat shaman in her kitchen. As she tried to get her head round the sudden strangeness of her life, the rat-man flashed her a smile so dazzling she stopped thinking and just smiled back. 'You try to understand and it is hard,' he agreed. 'But I like that you make the effort.' He drank his tea when she finished making it, hot water on leaves in a pot, not bags, and looked at her strangely. 'I think is a while since you did that,' he said. Masha had the odd idea that he was talking about making an effort, not about making proper tea, and she blushed.

She showed the rat-man where the rat sightings had been. Then he asked her to leave him to deal with them, so she left him to get on with the problem and sat back on the sofa. She tried staring into space but instead found herself thinking. Some of the conclusions she came to surprised her. When the rat-man knocked on her door to tell her he was going, she noticed the clock. Hours had passed.

'I think they won't come back no more,' said the rat-man. 'I have deal with them. And I see you try to deal with me. So I leave you this. Goodbye.' He tipped the brim of his rat-skull-encrusted hat at her, flashed another intoxicating grin and all but disappeared in a puff of smoke, kissing his fingers at her.

Masha looked at the folded paper he'd put into her hand. She was expecting a bill, but instead she saw a recipe in curly script. And a telephone number.

Masha put the recipe in a cookery book she hadn't used since domestic science at school. She didn't want it anywhere Joe might look. Then he came back, and as the rats had miraculously vanished, she didn't tell him anything about her adventure. It felt thrilling to have a secret which had nothing to do with him. But as her daily life returned to normal, she went back to turning herself into a human chemistry set. The

rats didn't put in any further appearances and her recent experiences merged into a haze, which she wasn't sure might not have been the product of her imagination.

Joe decided they ought to get married. His mother agreed with him. She liked Masha because she was slimmer than her daughter, less expensive, and apparently devoted to Joe. She thought Joe would do well to marry Masha so he would keep on getting his shirts ironed and such good food cooked. Between Joe and his mother, the wedding arrangements were stitched up. Masha looked at a lot of magazines with wedding dresses in them. It vaguely crossed her mind that she would look like an alien in the frocks, but it all seemed unreal to her anyway. With the wedding idea launched, Joe became proprietorial. He wanted to know what she was doing, what she was thinking, what she'd eaten at lunchtime. He phoned her at work every hour. She couldn't think of anything to say, but that didn't seem to bother him. He bought her things all the time. Gadgets for the home. Cute socks. Flowers. Chocolates. The odd ornament. He downloaded songs he thought she'd like, which she listened to as if they were in a foreign language.

He started making all sorts of reservations and pencilling in dates on the calendar like, Liberty's, Wedding List, 2.30pm, Possible Caterer, 4.30, and Florist, 12.15. The dates seemed far enough away not to matter at first, but gradually it dawned on Masha that they were becoming more real and more frightening, like the bars on the edge of a nightmare that gradually materialise into a prison. Masha woke one night to realise she'd been so occupied with pushing reality as far away from her as possible that she'd been backed into a corner. She lay quivering next to the inert Joe with her eyes stretched wide and her mouth in a rictus grin to stop her teeth from grinding. When Joe woke up, he found her next to him, wound tighter than a snare drum. 'You must be ready to come on,' he consoled her.

That night he brought her a handbook on dealing with painful periods. She threw it at him and locked herself in the kitchen. He shouted and battered on the door and pleaded with her to let him in. She curled up on a tea towel in the gap where the bin went. It wasn't until he left for work the next morning that she came out.

When he'd gone, she picked up the phone. She had a scrap of paper in her hand and she realised it was the only thing which could save her life.

Early that afternoon, the rat-man dropped round with a small parcel. He stayed for longer than it takes to drink several cups of coffee and when he left, he was empty handed. Masha spent what was left of the afternoon in the kitchen. The recipe wasn't one she'd ever used before, the handwriting was curly and hard to read and the ingredients were unfamiliar, and initially unpleasant to work with. But when she'd finished, she was pleased with the result.

Then she carefully checked she had the piece of paper with the address on it which she'd found on the dresser just after the rat-man departed, and left, empty-handed, locking the door carefully behind her. When she got to the end of the road, she dropped the key down a drain hole. As she turned the bend, she saw the cat sitting on the opposite pavement, staring at her impassively.

Masha gazed back but didn't stop walking. 'Are you coming too?' she asked. 'I haven't got the basket. You'll have to walk.' The cat bounded across the road and fell into step behind her. When Joe came home that night, he was surprised not to find Masha there, but reassured by the note she'd left on the table. It was the kind of simple message any nervous but house-proud bride-to-be might leave. Joe felt a rush of pride as he read what she'd put. In curlier than usual handwriting, it read Your Dinner Is In The Oven.

JOHNNY DOLL

We were known as the Ominous Cherubs because we looked cute and got away with murder. We weren't in a band because we couldn't play anything and when we sang, other people ran away. But we saw ourselves as Johnny Thunders' imaginary girlfriends, so we had an imaginary band as well, to put ourselves somewhere near his level. We hated the idea he might think we'd nothing better to do than just moon about over him.

Our names were Judy and Trudy Gonk, but in terms of our non-existent band, first we were Cack Attack, then the JuJu Slags and Ratwater Dog. That was after Penny, my Jack Russell, who'd swim after rodents in a nasty muddy pond in the woods at the bottom of Chapel Allerton park every time she got the chance. Ratwater Dog even had imaginary band t-shirts; we made them from matching rainbow vests and wore them to Reading Festival for Trudy's birthday. We ended up having our photo taken, pushing a shopping trolley filled with all our stuff, by Japanese tourists. We told them we were a famous band and they believed us. More fool them.

But in the end, we settled on calling ourselves the Ominous Cherubs, and sat around fluttering about Johnny and listening to his records. We loved Johnny. We loved the New York Dolls, the glam band of his glory days, but it was Johnny, solo, who touched the

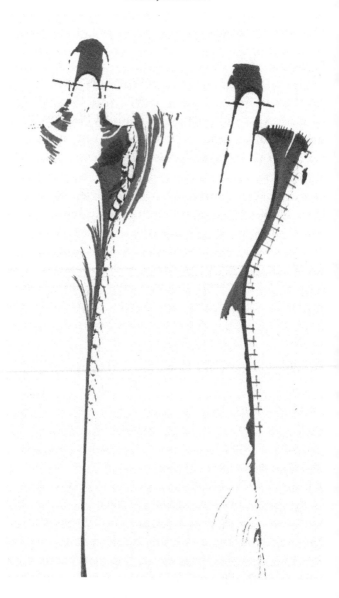

spot. Like us, he was spikey and pretty and whatever he did seemed doomed to disaster. He was playful when he wasn't comatose, and that was like us, too. Everything seemed like such an effort for him, and it was for us as well. We laughed at everything, but we had these heavy spirits we carted around with us, and we thought Johnny would understand. Of course we knew he was a hopeless falling down junkie but we had a soft spot for soft boys on drugs. We could care less. We were the Ominous Cherubs and Johnny was our doll.

He looked adorable and wrecked: great combination. He was light years out of it. He sang from a million miles away. He was a hopeless, doomed romantic without being sentimental: you can't put your arms around a memory, he sang. It made him all the more appealing, him being a defiant, gentle outlaw with a New York hard edge. That was missing in Leeds, which made him all the more heartbreaking.

He was Johnny Doll, and when he played his guitar and sang he was beautiful. He always wore good shoes, which was important, especially when walking the walk's the only thing you've got. He was born to lose, dressed to kill and hanging in there, barely by the skin of his teeth. Listen to the end of *So Alone*, after it sounds as if Johnny's given up, nodded out, faded into tragic oblivion. And then he comes back. His guitar speaking more eloquently than his cracked, shattered voice. First defiant, then exultant, then swaggering. Perfect.

Of course we knew the Johnny in our mind's eye was not the one who eked out a living trading on his former glories in the toilet venues which were the worn-out watering holes of England's decaying rock scene. We heard stories: Johnny dying on his feet on stage, his rare sets increasingly random, there being an ever-increasing likelihood of him not making it to the end. Johnny not being able to make it out of the dressing room. Johnny not turning up. But when we heard that Johnny was coming to the Duchess, it felt almost like a pilgrimage.

The Duchess was a seedy shrine of sorts. It was on the circuit; one of those venues which bands played when they were on the way up, to an audience of seen-it-all regulars. People would say, after the event, I saw so and so there before they made it, but chances are nobody was watching when the band was on. No-one played the Duchess when they'd got successful and gone on to bigger things, but once the glory days were over it welcomed them again like a resentful old friend from the days back when. It was dark in there and full of people who looked as if they'd been dug up.

We put our best shoes on because these things are important. Judy and Trudy Gonk, the Ominous Cherubs of Reginald Terrace, dressed in their best rags for Johnny. They were backcombed to blazes and lipsticked to the nines. When they poked their powdered noses through the door and picked their way through the flotsam, the usual crowd of people who'd never been out in daylight parted like a rock'n'roll Red Sea for us to take our positions at the front. In tribute to our own trash glamour we were placed as near to Johnny's spotlight as possible. We were all lit up and held each other's hands adoringly as we waited through the rubbish support act for Johnny to come and shine his love light on us.

Then there he was. But not the Johnny he was in our dreams. He was tiny, peaky, puzzled in his harem pants and a bowler hat. In our minds, he was Johnny Doll, and he was beautiful. But here was this wreck, shambling round on stage, not knowing where he was. He couldn't remember his songs. He'd play a bit, sing a line or two, stop, forget the rest. He knew he was meant to do something but he couldn't remember what it was. He'd wander into the wings and look at us with unfocused eyes in his little green-white face as if we were a problem he couldn't solve. He didn't see Trudy and Judy even if no one else could miss us. He was beyond seeing us. We loved him all the more for it.

We loved him with all our hearts, clinging to each other's hands, willing Johnny on as he faltered and died on stage for what must have been the millionth time in his lost lifetime. But we were the only ones with any compassion that night. They turned on him. Johnny was jeered at by a crowd of brickies in lipstick who'd only turned up in the hope that this might be the night Johnny would die for real. If he couldn't sing and play them his sublime narcotic lullabies, they wanted his blood.

'Come on Johnny, play us your guitar,' the ghouls taunted, as it hung around his neck, an untouched, unwieldy foreign object. He looked at it from miles away. He didn't know where he was.

He couldn't see them, but there they were, mocking him. Standing in stolid self-righteousness, they were school bullies with fat legs, a million miles from Johnny's fragile bird bones, crammed into skin-tight black jeans. Their black leather jackets bulged over beer bellies, not hung from coat-hanger shoulders. Tee shirts were stretched over barrel chests instead of Johnny's ironing-board frame.

They were merciless. It was like watching a rag doll being torn apart by cruel children who'd outgrown a beloved plaything. You could hear them, their northern voices thickened by cheap beer and cigarettes, sneering at the man they'd modelled themselves on.

It was horrible. The more the catcalls came, the more Johnny disintegrated. We couldn't bear to watch as he forgot his words, wandered off stage, came back again. We went to the back and out of love, we tried not to watch. We wanted to cry but we weren't left alone.

'I call him Johnny Blunders.' It was the thick-voiced singer from the going-nowhere support act. He leered at Trudy and me because we were the kind of dolly girls no-hopers like him wanted hanging off their arms. We wouldn't have touched him with a bargepole. He'd never begin to know the heights of

Johnny's glory. But he was right. We hated him for it, but Johnny was past his sell-by date.

Johnny died in New Orleans a couple of years after that. He'd hung on longer than anyone had expected but no-one was surprised at the news. All his shoes were stolen. No-one ever found out who'd taken them. It took the Duchess almost a decade to close down but that was as inevitable as Johnny's demise. No-one went to see bands in small venues and glorious rock'n'roll failure, as a lifestyle, was as much a stiff as those, like Johnny, who'd lived it and died it and made it a legend that no-one wanted to act out any more. The Duchess was like Johnny: it went into a terminal decline, passed out and then passed away. I don't know where the ghouls went that haunted it, but Judy and Trudy Gonk, the Ominous Cherubs, are still going. Unlike many of rock'n'roll's finest, they weren't a short-lived act.

Johnny stopped being our doll that night at the Duchess. It wasn't that we didn't love him but we wanted to imagine him as he used to be, and we couldn't any more. Johnny said it himself. You can't put your arms around a memory. You can't see it in clear detail, either. I couldn't tell you, for instance, what shoes any of us were wearing that night, though it seemed important at the time. But it never fades away; quite often it comes back. And it haunts you.

HOOPING THE GIRL

Onstage or off, Pa wore a gold lame shirt to make sure the limelight shone wherever he was standing. He didn't take prisoners, Pa, least of all himself. No downtime. No slacking. No sleeping on the job, even if it was one of those jobs that didn't seem to make any kind of difference. Where other folks saw everyday life, Pa saw an endless procession of opportunities to make sure he never ended up back where he came from, sharing a mud floor with eight siblings in a village where there was no running water and no way out, or at least not one that was signposted.

Pa was never going to be any old bicycle acrobat: he was going to be the one people remembered. 'When they think they're amazed – make sure the next thing you do astounds them,' he'd say. 'Takes the breath right out of their bodies so they don't believe what they're seeing.'

Pa said he had to work harder because he was one of the People which meant he had more to prove and Ma had to work harder because she wasn't, so he expected her to fall short, and us kids had to work harder because there were no half-and-half passengers in our family, but the truth was we all had to work harder because he was mean down to the smallest bone in his body. There are snakes less mean than Pa. Even the wasps knew they'd met their match in the meanness stakes, and they

never once pestered him. He got the idea for my act from watching people trying to win goldfish on the Midway. Throwing hoops over the fishbowls. When I was eleven, the age for me to have my own role in the show, Pa trained me by throwing hoops over me.

When he aimed those hoops, they came fast. The first one cracked my cheekbone and when I ducked for the second, the third nearly scalped me. The fourth one I got inside but he'd thrown it with such force I was nearly strangled. By the fifth hoop it was war, and I wasn't going to be beaten like my Ma. I got inside that darn hoop and I kept it going. And the next, and the one after that. He kept those hoops coming until the fire burned down and there was no more light to see where he was throwing.

I was Princess Hula Lei, all the way from Hawaii. I'd hook a single hoop with my toes, and get it started, and once that was going, round my ankles, I'd hook another, and get the first one travelling up as far as my knees. And then Pa would start aiming hoops at me so they landed over my head 'til I was inside them all, which is when the ones going up would meet the ones going down, all the way up my body, and I'd reach inside then start spinning hoops at the end of each wrist. We got it up to nineteen. Not bad for a kid, but not good enough for Pa.

Nothing ever was. He wasn't just a perfectionist. He drove me, and Jimmy, and Ma so hard that the other acts would all have gone to bed, lights out in their trailers, whilst he was still working us. 'Radu, they're kids, let them sleep', Ma would plead, but Pa would cut her short. 'They can sleep when they've earned it', he would say, and if she persisted, he'd answer her back with his fist, though never in a place that wouldn't be covered up by her costume when it was showtime.

He never said if you'd done well. 'Tell your Ma to get your costume made up for tomorrow's show', he growled once I'd added the twentieth hoop. I crawled up the trailer steps to find the bottle of witch hazel my Ma used. And like he always did, Pa swaggered into the dark where there was liquor, and the kind of dames who looked into his black eyes and saw romance, and not, like Ma, nothing but their own dead-eyed reflection.

Pa may not have shown that he liked it, but the audiences did. Little Princess Hula Lei, with her gutsy smile and her tough elastic body, free of distracting women's lumps and bumps, was well set to becoming an attraction in her own right. She was meant to be an interlude between Pa's first set of tricks and his finale, but she got to be enough of a draw that Management started talking about giving her a spot of her own. Not that anyone said anything direct to me but it's hard to keep secrets in a place where the only walls are tents and trailers. 'Get the kid up on the bill', drawled High Lee the ringmaster. 'Fresh blood brings new bites. Stops the old stuff feeling like the same old same old'.

You should have seen Pa's face, but he never opened his mouth. He just set to – working on his own with that bike 'til he got it so he was doing tricks with it that would have seemed impossible if you hadn't seen it with your own eyes. Backwards backflips. Sideways spins. He got it up to racing speed, stood on the handlebars, did a triple somersault and landed in the saddle. He made it dance the polka.

The audiences loved it. Pa took their breath away.

But they loved Princess Hula Lei even more.

So after every show, Pa needed to take it out on someone. He took it out on Jimmy by never saying a word to him beyond get this and fetch that. And every morning Ma's eyes showed that he'd found a new way to take it out on her.

He took it out on me by working me harder and harder. 'Even if you get it up to twenty-five, you're

just another hoop act,' he said, sneering like I was something he'd found on his shoe. But then he came up with the trick that would make seeing into not quite believing.

Once I'd got twenty hoops going, a wire was lowered from the rigging, and I gripped on to it with my teeth. Then, with all twenty hoops a-spinning, I got pulled right up towards the apex of the big top. It was only when I looked like a tiny doll suspended all that way over the sawdust that Pa would let me stop hooping, so that golden circles fell onto the sawdust from a great height, and the audience nearly turned themselves inside out with cheering.

When that happened, Pa didn't need to say anything. I'd lived up to his expectations. Everyone knew it and everyone knew that it was all down to him that I'd done it. Management got new posters printed with The Spinning Maximoffs right at the top of the bill, and wheels and hoops all the way down the sides. There was a while when he didn't take anything out on anyone. He even got to smiling at Ma once or twice.

We lived like that for several weeks, and the show kept moving on.

Then came the matinee when Ma messed up Pa's finale. It involved a set-up and it had to be precise: four raised platforms positioned by Ma where Pa would flip the bike backwards into a roll before moving on seamlessly to the next one. On a good night, which was every night, round and round he'd go, a golden blur of man and machine. But Ma slipped up that afternoon when she misplaced one of the platforms and instead of that bike twisting and turning round the ring, the front wheel missed its mark and the bike tumbled to the ground with Pa beneath it.

Pa picked himself off the ground, got back on the bike. And tried again.

And fell again.

Four times Pa got back on the bike, and it didn't feel like a family day out under that big top. It felt like someone was on trial for his life. When he finally made the complete turning circle and left the ring, everyone let out their breath and wiped their foreheads. But no-one clapped, and High Lee sent in the clowns an act early.

Ma wore make up the next day to cover the bruises, though they still showed through. But she put Pa's breakfast in front of him without saying a word, and I knew from way down inside me that she never would. I knew there would never be a time when she'd stop paying for something she didn't even know was a mistake 'til it was too late.

She saw me looking and her eyes told me to be silent. I bit my tongue. But later, when Pa was gone, she said one thing to me.

'I chose this. That doesn't mean it has to be this way for you. And I don't want it to be. But you have to make it happen.'

I looked at her. Ma was soft. I loved her, so much it hurt, but I was different from her.

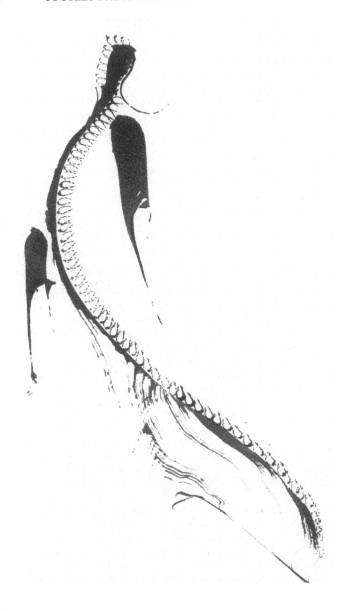

That night it was business as usual. Pa's routine went off without a hitch 'til the midpoint, which is when Princess Hula Lei came on. I got those hoops spinning just like I always did, taking particular care because I wanted to remember the look on Pa's face as he landed each one over me. Except there wasn't a look. Pa was like a machine, shooting hoops at his daughter like we were on a construction line.

When the wire came down, he went to clip the safety onto me and I shrugged him off.

'This time it's not for show. It's for real,' I told him, just before the roustabouts started hauling me up to the apex of that big top with all those hoops still turning and turning. And for a split second, before I flew into the air, I saw a look in his eyes that told me I'd earned his respect. That I was my father's daughter.

I got as far as the wire would go and I kept right on going. When the wire ran out I span on and on,

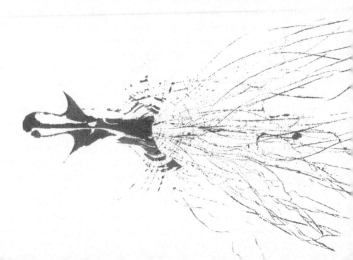

shooting onwards and upwards through the hole in the top of the tent in a blazing blur of brightness. I wasn't Princess Hula Lei any more. I was a shooting star.

The next day, there were reports of a meteor that travelled across the sky, pulsing with a golden glow as it passed over the big top, over the tents and trailers, and then traveled on its way to who knows where.

It wasn't a meteor. But if you look up on a dark night, perhaps when the circus comes to town, there's a chance – a rare one, mind – that you might see me. I'm not saying you'll believe what's before your eyes, but I haven't yet let a single hoop fall to the ground.

WHY THERE IS NO
LONGER ANY BOREK

From time to time, Dolores liked to pack a carpet bag with the bare necessities - toothpaste, tippet, gin, an emergency Marmite sandwich - and set out on her travels. She always packed light, to leave room in the carpet bag for the souvenirs she knew would find their way, somehow, into its capacious depths.

On this particular occasion, she headed past the land where deep, dark woods sheltered bears and wolves, through the land beyond the forest – where she was tempted to stop, because the music set her toes tap-tap-tapping – to a place where the sun shone so brightly that field after field of sunflowers turned their faces to the warmth and the air smelt dry and spiced.

She followed her nose in the direction the spicy smell took her, and found herself on the outskirts of a village. In the distance she heard the strange, sinuous sound of a wind instrument, set to the irresistible beating of a drum. So as well as following her nose, Dolores began to follow her ears. And then, in the distance, she saw people waving at her in greeting, so she followed her eyes too, and marched up to them.

The music – it was definitely music, but with a wonky rhythm, and not a tune that Dolores had heard before – got stronger and stronger as she got

nearer and nearer, and the people waved at her and smiled. She smoothed down her frock – even when travelling, Dolores dressed for an occasion, because you never know when one might turn up.

'Who are these people? What is this music? Is this a party?'

'It is a wedding party,' the people told her. 'And you have brought extra luck to the happy couple by arriving at this village in time for the marriage. So you must join us, and dance for the bride and groom.'

Dolores was always delighted to shake a leg, whether it was for love or for money, so she let herself be swept up by the welcoming villagers into their dancing circle. Round and round they went, and round and round again, all the way round the village, holding hands and dancing to a song that had no beginning she could make out, and seemed to have no end, either. Round and round they went, and round and round again, until the sun, which had been in the middle of the sky when they started, slid down below the horizon and vanished completely out of sight. So round and round they danced, in the dark, until Dolores came to a halt.

She was hungry.

She hadn't eaten since breakfast, and now it was well past dinner time.

''Is there anything to eat? I'm feeling a bit peckish.'

At the sound of her voice, the man who played the wind instrument and the man who played the drum stopped blowing and banging, and the village fell silent.

The man who played the wind instrument went to stand on Dolores' right side. He had a handsome moustache.

'This woman is magnificent. She will be my future wife.'

Quickly, the man who played the drum went to stand on her left side. His moustache was a thing of splendour.

'This woman is incomparable. She will be MY future wife.'

Dolores glared at them both.

'My stomach thinks my throat's been cut.' She was one of those people that got cranky when she was hungry, and by this point she was very hungry indeed.

The two musicians and the rest of the village looked at her curiously, uncertain what she meant.

'Feed me!' she roared, and mimed stuffing her face with food.

At that, there was a hustle and a bustle, a flurry and a scurry, and a woman in a headscarf came bustling towards her with an enormous tray of pie.

'For the future wife of my son Ferus the clarinet player, I am honoured to offer you my finest borek.'

She laid the tray in front of Dolores, who cut a tiny square and bit a tiny bite, nibbling delicately on the corner. As the borek's delicious flavours - the fatty, salty, cheesy, doughy flavours - invaded her tastebuds, she smiled at the woman a smile of deep appreciation.

Then, while the woman was congratulating herself on what a charming, well-mannered daughter-in-law she was getting, Dolores snatched up the entire borek with both hands and began to cram it into her mouth.

Soon it was all gone. Not even a flaky crumb was left.

'That was nice,' said Dolores. 'Doesn't touch the sides though. Is there any more?'

Sadly the woman shook her head. Dolores had consumed a borek big enough to feed a whole family, including the great-great-grandmother.

Another woman in a headscarf came rushing up, as fast as she could, carrying a tray of pie so vast she staggered under the weight of it, and directed her remarks at the first woman.

'No wonder the poor thing is still famished. Everyone in the village knows you are a terrible cook and all your guests go hungry. Watch MY son's future wife. She will soon be satisfied when she eats the borek I am famous for.'

She laid her tray at Dolores' feet, and the smell of salty cheese, greasy pastry, spinach and spices made Dolores' mouth water. She reached down, folded the entire borek into an enormous triangle, and wedged the whole thing in her mouth.

When she had chewed and swallowed, she burped gently.

'That was delicious. More, please.'

But there wasn't any more.

The first headscarfed woman laughed in triumph.

'I will show you how well I will provide for my future daughter in law', she said, and disappeared into the village. In a matter of minutes she returned, her arms and the arms of her many relatives piled up with all the borek that had been provided for the wedding feast, and laid it at Dolores' feet.

'I definitely need more than a small snack,' said Dolores, settling on the ground so she was nearer to her food. And before you could say 'who ate all the pies?' Dolores had eaten all the pies.

'That was great. I could go on eating that all night. Please may I have some more?'

But there wasn't any more. Dolores had eaten all the borek in the village.

The second headscarfed woman - the mother of the drummer, who was looking at Dolores with great admiration, and licking his lips beneath his moustache - folded her arms.

'You must come with me. My village, which will be your home when you have married my son Saban, is famous for its borek. There, we appreciate a woman with a good appetite. There will be all the borek you could possibly want, and more.'

But there wasn't. Because as fast as they brought borek to her, Dolores ate it. She ate cheese borek, spinach borek and meat borek. She ate it from plates, she ate it from dishes and she ate it straight out of the pan. She ate all the borek in the village, and when she had eaten it, she wiped her lips and smiled politely and said: 'That was delicious. Please may I have some more?'

'We cannot let her go hungry! Or she will not marry my son!'

When she had eaten all the borek in the valley, Dolores ate all the borek in the province, and still she asked for more. The woman sent donkeys with carts to the big town, and they came back laden with borek, and Dolores ate that, too. So the carts were sent to the next town, and the one after that, until all the towns and villages had given up all their borek, and Dolores ate it up until all the borek had gone.

'Help a girl out here,' she said. 'I'm still ravenous.'

But there was no borek left to feed her on.

So the woman clipped her son Saban round the ear and told him to find a bride he could afford to feed on a musician's wages. And Saban looked dolefully at Dolores, sitting on the hillside with her lips greasy from eating all the borek, and he sighed deeply because he knew no skinny girl could ever match Dolores in her magnificence. And then, with his moustaches drooping, he strapped his drum round his neck and set off to earn the money to buy flour, and cheese, and oil, and spices, so that his mother could - when the ingredients became available again - make more borek.

As for Dolores, she picked up her carpet bag and went on her way. She didn't feel a bit sorry about Saban the drummer and Ferus the clarinet player who had both wanted to be her husband. There was a gentleman caller waiting for her in the land beyond the land beyond the forest, and when no-one had been looking, she'd tucked an entire borek in her bag for him. But as she walked, it struck her that she was still quite hungry. So she ate it.

Still not enough borek to feed Dolores

Phyllo pastry	6,000 sheets
Eggs	1,000
Yoghurt	100 barrels
Milk	10 barrels
Oil	100 barrels
Leeks, chopped	1,000
Courgette, chopped	1,000
Spinach, chopped	450 kilos
Nutmeg	500 grammes
Salt	500 grammes
Pepper	500 grammes
Boreklik combi beyaz	350 kilos
Feta	400 kilos
Forest herbs, dried at moonlight	1 bushel
Forest twigs, to scatter	1 bushel

CLARICE

Clarice was a psychic, but it wasn't something she would have chosen for herself. Her mother earned her living as a medium, working at the end of a pier in a chilly northern seaside resort. Her work, and her person, were an embarrassment to her daughter, who aspired to something more respectable for herself than the dyed jet corkscrew curls, cheerful bad taste and phenomenal ability to foresee the future of her parent.

Ada liked a drink, loved dolling herself up to go dancing, wasn't above egging strange men on and had a reputation for being a card. Clarice, never what you might call a lively child, cringed inwardly every night when her mother came back from the pier, cast off her mouldy old squirrel-skin and poured her usual milk stout into a tea cup in case the neighbours were watching, all the time recounting tales wherein the dead mingled with the living and conversed, if anything, more freely than those smitten with grief who were left behind.

Clarice wanted nothing of it. She yearned for a world where only what was visible was real. In her mother's home, you were never alone even if you were there by yourself, and Ada and the spirit presences being companionable, you had to put up with overhearing endless conversations, which to anybody who didn't know, would seem as if her mother was incessantly talking to herself.

The boundaries between life and death were very fuzzy to open-hearted, extrovert Ada. As a child, Clarice simply accepted that unseen voices came into their presence and said things that sometimes made sense, and other times, didn't. There was one old woman who used to tell Clarice off whenever she hid from Ada in the cellar. The old woman told her over and over again that if she weren't careful, she'd marry a man who would collect guns and come to a bad end. Invisible twin girls played with her in the attic, and in the back bedroom, the ghost of drunken Mr Higginshaw would rant and rave and ask Clarice to show him her drawers. 'Come and sit on my lap,' he'd cajole, but Clarice could never see any knees to sit on.

When she told her schoolmates about the unseen inhabitants of her house, they laughed at her, nicknamed her 'Barmy Bertha' and sneaked on her to the teacher. Miss Harmsworth scolded her in front of the class for telling lies. Bitterly humiliated, Clarice learned that what she'd inherited from Ada was a source of shame, not pride, and from then on she kept her mouth shut.

After that, she rigidly suppressed anything about herself that might make her stand out from the crowd. If the voices came, she ignored them as much as possible. She never let on that anything out of the ordinary ever happened to her. She was a solid, heavy-set girl and it was relatively easy for her to seem as ordinary as she wished she were. Using her mother as a yardstick for everything she wanted to reject, she moved slowly, discouraged the attentions of all but the most stolidly respectable young men, and got herself a sensible job in accounts once she left school. As soon as a suitable young man asked her, she married him and gratefully moved out of her flighty mother's disorganised house.

At first, there was only herself and Alfred in the terraced stone cottage, and Clarice was quietly, deliriously happy. The very dullness of their routine thrilled her: she loved being an orderly housewife paired to a man whose monotone solemnity was a delight after Ada's incessantly melodramatic presence. Clarice threw herself into her welcome new life, and for many years everything continued without a hitch.

The day Alfred brought the gun home was a turning point. He'd fund it in a junk shop. It was ancient, grimy, and to Clarice, not worth bothering with. Nonetheless, Alfred was fascinated and sat at the kitchen table until well past his usual bedtime, lovingly cleaning and polishing the thing until it gleamed. Under his gentle hands, it glowed with antique beauty: its dark, gleaming wood shone with a resurrected patina offset by heavily engraved brass work. It was definitely a thing of beauty: Alfred acted like a man who had found his passion. Clarice had never seen him so lit up. She went to bed and left him sitting in a state of enchantment, holding his gun in his hands with more tenderness than he'd ever shown towards her. She couldn't find it in her heart to be jealous of a silly gun, but all the same her heart sank. As she moved down the passage towards the bedroom, she heard a voice. Plain as plain could be, it was, saying, 'I told you this would happen.' It was the old woman from the attic in her mother's house.

That night, as Clarice lay awake, she could hear voices speaking to her from all over the house. Some of their words were indistinct; others plain as punch. 'Clarice, Clarice,' she heard. 'Clarice, let us in. We're not here to hurt you, Clarice. We only want to talk to you. We're here to be company for you, Clarice, now that he won't. He doesn't know you like we do, Clarice. We've known you ever since you were little. We'll keep you company, Clarice. We've got all sorts to tell you.' She couldn't sleep for the onslaught of voices, all telling her they they'd missed her, that they were glad she'd let them back in. 'You need us, Clarice. You can't shut us out. We're not outsiders Clarice, you're one of us. You can't deny your own,' she heard, even when she hid under the bedclothes. Beside her, the slumbering Alfred snored on, oblivious. The voices were so loud that Clarice didn't know how anybody could sleep through such a racket.

As the voices didn't go away, Clarice resigned herself to them. They told her all sorts about the neighbours. Some of it was useful and all of it she would have preferred to keep to herself. Even so, following the time when Clarice inadvertently asked when Mrs Jones' mother's funeral was taking place before being told that the old lady had passed away, people began to wonder if she might know something they didn't. It wasn't long before surreptitiously casual visitors would ask her how their dear departed were getting on in the next world. Try as she might to keep her mouth shut, sometimes a voice would sneak through, using her as a mouthpiece. Reluctantly, Clarice was forced to admit that she'd inherited her mother's formidable powers and deal with what that meant in terms of other people's insatiable curiosity about the afterlife.

Sometimes the voices pre-empted her conscience. They came out with things she would rather have kept to herself. When Wendy Smith's Harry came back across the great divide to tell her how glad he was to have passed on since it spared him the sight of her face like a hen's bottom every day God sent, Clarice could have gone through the floor. Because her predictions were always remarkably accurate, and because she scrupulously refused to embroider what she knew, everybody believed that what she'd said was gospel. It wasn't long after that Mrs Smith went to join her eldest daughter Tamsin in Australia.

Being a kindly soul, Clarice helped those seeking her advice if she was asked, although her own response to her ability was still to conceal it as much as possible. She hated to be regarded as 'the medium' like some local curiosity, avoided the topic of the afterlife at social events and never charged a penny for contacting the other side, treating it as a favour between neighbours. In fact, she took great pains to present the appearance that everything was normal – just as it should be.

Still, as Alfred's interest in collecting old guns grew into an obsessive hobby, the voices were company for her. Although she'd have never let on to a soul, she was secretly pleased that there were people to go home to. They were interested in her comings and goings; she dearly loved a gossip and the flesh and blood people she knew couldn't be approached on terms of such intimacy because her strange powers, coupled with her reticent manners, set her rather apart. She was respected, even liked, but familiar with no-one outside the spirit community. As the years passed, the spirits became more real to her than anyone in the physical world had ever been.

Things change, but sometimes the process is so imperceptible that they seem to be set in stone. Clarice's life remained the same for so long that she was sure the routine she followed would carry on until the last trumpet sounded. Therefore, she was in her sixties, and unprepared, when Alfred shot his leg off whilst cleaning his gun collection, and consequently died. This event, which the voices had not warned her about, was followed by a rapid succession of events, which turned her life upside-down.

She met Jim and fell in love for the first time ever, remarried, set up in the antiques business and discovered that she adored dressing up and going out dancing with her burly, gregarious husband. She was too busy, and happy, to listen to her voices, so they went away completely. Clarice didn't have time to miss them. She was so busy talking to Jim that she didn't even realise they weren't there any more.

They didn't come back even when Jim died and Clarice could dearly have done with their company. She missed Jim more than she could ever have imagined, but try as she might, she couldn't reach him on the other side or get in touch with anybody who could reassure her that he was happy in the afterlife. It took every ounce of willpower she possessed to stop herself from falling to pieces.

For the first time ever, she was completely alone. It was harder than she'd ever expected. She'd come into her own late in life, and bravely, was determined to make the most of it before old age made it impossible.

Jim, who'd come into her life at an age when most people's partners are fading out, had given her the confidence to realise that anything is possible. She hated being alone but was determined to make the best of it. As she'd been too busy in her early life making herself anonymous to do anything that really pleased her, she made up her mind to do whatever took her fancy before it was too late. If Jim had given her anything, it was the belief in herself that comes with being truly loved.

So, she travelled. She went to Scotland, and Cornwall, and the Isle of Wight. While she was there, she made every effort to find company, male for preference. She liked her escorts to be dancing partners. She took herself abroad, and then on a cruise. Nobody ever replaced her Jim, but she enjoyed the company of her gentleman friends, who made up for the flirtations she's never had as a girl. She grew to prize her independence and realised there was as much point in doing things for herself as there was in doing them for other people. In her late seventies, Clarice was a happier, jollier and more fulfilled woman than the young girl she had been could ever have imagined.

On her last trip, she took herself to Brighton. She went alone, planning to spend a few days pottering around the lanes looking for junk and curios. She was happy alone, exploring every nook and cranny, hoping to unearth some exciting small find which would make her trip worthwhile. Every shop she entered she went over with a fine-toothed comb. Clarice was in her element.

What slipped her notice was a sign in one of the windows that said 'Tarot'. It was only when Clarice was at the back of the shop that she noticed the deck of cards spread out in front of a young woman sitting at a table in an alcove. The images were familiar to her from her childhood: Ada had consulted them daily in both personal and professional capacities. Clarice had been used to her mother postponing activities because the Hanged Man had shown up, or suddenly pack a bag and take off at a tangent because the Chariot suggested a journey was in the offing. Maybe it was

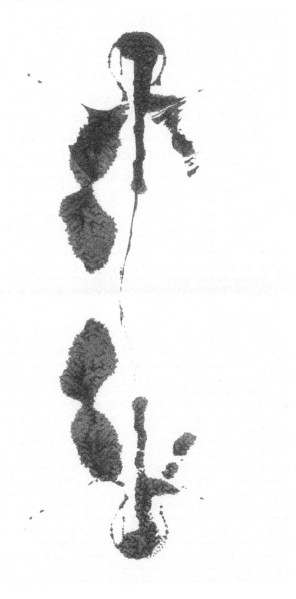

nostalgia that prompted Clarice towards the cards; maybe after all the years she had finally accepted her mother for what she had been. Maybe it was simple curiosity. Clarice had had no dealings with the supernatural for fifteen years. Perhaps she just wanted to see if there was still anything there.

Whatever her motives, she asked the young woman if she would read her fortune for her. Smilingly, the woman passed her the cards, and asked Clarice to shuffle them.

As Clarice touched the cards, an intense feeling of sickness overwhelmed her. As she shuffled and cut, the feeling grew. Clarice was sure she would faint. She passed the cards back to their owner and surrendered to the band of choking nausea that pressed into her throat. Dimly, as if from miles away, she was aware that the woman was laying the cards down in time-honoured ritual placings, but she couldn't hear what she was saying.

The sensation that she was being strangled became more extreme. Clarice needed all her concentration to make sure she didn't succumb to it and stop breathing. Fighting sickness, blinding lights and the dizzy sensation that she was spinning and falling at the same time, she used every ounce of willpower to retain a hold on the life that felt as if it was being sucked out of her.

The young woman came to the end of her reading and put the cards away. For the first time, she looked directly at Clarice, who was vainly trying to disguise the fact that she was gasping for breath, although beginning to feel a bit better. 'Are you not very well?' asked the Tarot reader of her purple-faced client. It took Clarice a few moments to answer that no, she had come over very peculiar but it was passing, thank you. Kindly, the woman asked if she'd taken in any of the reading. No, replied Clarice, she'd felt too unwell to concentrate. She'd heard nothing. The woman offered to retell Clarice's fortune, and got her a glass of water.

Clarice, perturbed by her funny turn, was thankful it seemed to have passed so quickly. She drank her water slowly, and by the end of the glass, felt as right as rain. She reached out her hands for the pack of cards, and the woman placed them in her hands. The moment she began to finger the deck, the sick, choking feeling engulfed her.

'I can't do this,' mouthed Clarice, roughly thrusting the pack towards its owner. 'Whatever's happening to me is coming from them.'

Their owner looked horrified. She'd started reading the cards when a friend gave her a deck; had learned about the meanings attached to the ancient images from a book with illustrations. She read by rote rather than exercising her imagination and nothing strange or untoward had ever happened to her while she was reading the cards. She was the first to admit she was no clairvoyant, although she had a definite facility for helping people with problems of an emotional nature when they wanted to talk them through.

Mediumship is a bit like riding a bike: once you get the hang of it, you never forget how it's done. Things

were stirring in Clarice that had been dormant for a decade and a half. 'Who last touched these cards?' she asked, but already she knew, and would have preferred not to. There was a man hanging suspended from a light fitting in an over-furnished kitchen. His neck was broken, eyes bulging, tongue protruding.

'It was his wife who found him,' she whispered. 'She came to you the day he did it. She wanted to know if she should stay with him, or go with her fancy man. You told her to follow her heart. He was dead when she got back home. Did it while she was sitting here. He was trying to get through to her.'

Clarice looked up. The Tarot reader was white and shaking. 'I'm sorry love,' said Clarice. 'You'd best get rid of them.' She patted the stricken girl on the arm. 'It doesn't do to take it too personally,' she added kindly. That's what Ada always used to say whenever the spirits told her something unpleasant. You can't get involved or you'd never have a life of your own, she'd tell Clarice.

Well, Clarice did have a life of her own but she wasn't sorry they'd come back to keep her company. She could have done without the shock, but once it was over it was good to feel she wasn't too alone any more. She fetched the girl a glass of water and walked out into the street. 'Clarice, Clarice,' said a voice in her ear. She looked around, although she knew there was nobody to see, and smiled.

LALLY

I first saw Lally when she was coming across the gardens outside the Blue Mosque. She didn't so much walk, as shimmer. All the edges of her – hair, skin, the long silky shift she was wearing – were softened in the heat haze of a steamy Istanbul summer, so that she seemed to be melting into the sun. Or walking out of it. A golden girl walking out of the golden sun. As she made her way towards the Pudding Shop, Rob's face wore the beatific expression of a mystic being graced with a vision.

I need to go back a bit. In England – in Pinner – at the beginning of the 1970s, life was still black and white. Like the 1950s. Like an Ealing comedy, only without the fun. Where we lived, there were neat houses, with neat gardens, and neat lives were lived in them. If you were middle-class, like we were, the revolutions of the 1960s barely touched Pinner. It was conservative, respectable, and well-off. For people like me and Rob, who were young, and had dreams, and wanted to see the world in colour, living in Pinner was like being buried alive.

Up the road, though, in Harrow, there were squats graffitied with slogans like 'your logic is a dog and so am I' and pubs where you could score. When Rob got into art college there, he found what he wanted to find. He grew his hair. He threw himself into the scene. His friends weren't the other students on his course, but the freaks and stoners he met in town. There were parties, all-nighters, gigs, festivals. He was rarely home. 'It's freedom, Ju-Ju-man,' he told me, high and intent. He'd even changed my name: no-one else ever called me that. He poured everything into living that life. There were no half-measures with Rob, there never had been. Like when he was a kid and he got into dinosaurs, or the Ancient Egyptians. They weren't interests, they were obsessions.

The first sign that something was amiss came when he showed me his portfolio. As he opened out the pictures, colour sprawled in fractals across the pages, fragmented, disjointed, not making sense. 'Is there a theme to this?' I asked, trying to understand what I was looking at. 'It's the extensions, Ju-Ju-man, the things that get built on to house the bits of your brain that fall out.' He was giggling, grinning, talking rubbish, but at the time I put it down to the hash and I wasn't too bothered about it. I smoked too, and dug hanging out, records, and bands, but I'd just got three As in my A'levels and been offered a place at Durham to do PPE. The dope opened everything out. Made things possible. Durham! I'd be the first person in our family to get to uni.

I was in a lecture when Mother rang. There was a message at the porter's lodge and I called her back. Dad had only just stopped Rob from jumping off the top of the garage roof and he'd been sectioned. It wasn't Mother's style to get hysterical but she sounded worried. 'He's not making any sense and the only thing we can think of is that he must have taken something. Do you know if he takes drugs, Julian? If you do, then you must tell us.'

But I didn't. He'd have just been high. Maybe a bit too high. But he was living his truth. I'd read Ronnie Laing, though that wasn't something the parents would be able to handle. Drugs were the bogeyman for our parents' generation. They wanted Pinner, not the wide world.

And now Rob was locked up. In Shenley. When we were kids, we'd tease each other with its name when we knew our games were getting a bit too wild for Mother.

I hitched down as soon as I'd finished my last seminar on Friday.

'What's going on, Rob?' His hair had mushroomed but beneath it there was an absence in his eyes and jumpiness to the rest of him that made me understand that something was very wrong with my brother.

'Heavy shit, Ju-Ju-man. In my head. I got out of it but they followed me here. You won't let them get me, will you, Ju-Ju-man? You won't let them, will you?'

'I won't let anything hurt you, Rob,' I promised. I stroked his arms until he stopped shaking, and I realised that even though he was two years older than me, I was the big brother now.

Rob did well when he got out of hospital. He didn't go back to art college, but lived at home and got a job he liked, in Pinner Park. He'd calmed down a lot, and seemed chilled and happy with a quiet life.

One of his tasks was looking after the ornamental fish, and the parakeets, and when I was home for the holidays I used to hang out with him, enjoying his peaceful company and gentle chat about the places he'd journey to, one of these days. Afghanistan. India. Nepal. He had no firm travel plans in mind, just a litany of magical names. Manali. Herat. Kathmandu. He knew all the routes; all the places.

'When are you off, then, Rob?'

'When it's time,' he'd say, with a faraway look in his eyes. 'When it's time to go.' But he seemed content with his park, and his fish, and his parakeets, and hanging out with the friends he'd made in Harrow. He didn't seem to want for much. I did. I wanted to get out, move on. See things, do things. I'd just graduated, and was applying for teacher training. I was a doer. Rob was one of life's dreamers. 'Not a dreamer, Ju-Ju-man,' he corrected me gently. 'A seeker.'

'I'm going to India.' When it came, he said the words quite calmly, as if there was nothing unexpected to them. 'Overland. I'm setting off in August.'

Of course there was an outcry. Mother went white and Dad said that he refused to allow it. Rob was shaken, but adamant.

'It's time. I need to go east,' he said. 'I need to find the answers. I'm looking for something, and it's time for me to find it.'

Dad put his foot down. 'I will not permit you to go. You live in my house and you will obey my rules.'

The next time Rob came downstairs, there was absence in his eyes and anxiety round his mouth. Mother saw it too.

'You've been ill,' Mother pleaded.

'The journey does not stop because of an obstacle in the road,' Rob told her. 'I need to find the answers.'

He picked at his nails and hair, and wouldn't eat. I heard him pacing in his room long after the rest of the family had gone to bed.

It went on for days. Dad angry, Mother begging, Rob determined.

'I'll go with him,' I announced. 'I'll keep an eye on him.' It meant me putting off teacher training to the following year but what the hell? I was young, it was time for some fun, and vagabonding overland to Nepal sounded a fine adventure.

There were conditions. We had to book an itinerary, and be back by Christmas.

On the Bargain Bus, Rob was a tranquil presence amidst the eager long-haulers, listening to his cassette player, occasionally smoking a joint if there was one going round, and showing no signs of excitement as the painted coach ate up the long miles through Yugoslavia. 'Take it easy, Ju-Ju-man,' he smiled as I beat him to the window seat. 'The journey doesn't start til we get to Istanbul.'

We headed straight for the Pudding Shop and walked into another world. I just sat and stared – not at the domed skyline, or the crowds in the streets, though I'd never seen anything like it – but at the longhairs, free-wheelers, hippies and freaks who lined the walls and packed out the tables, talking in different languages, dressed in exotic, colourful clothes. I'd met people who had done the trail, of course I had, but nothing had prepared me for this meeting of the tribes. Rob might have been there all his life. He fit right in, talking to people, making connections. That night we had a lump of pollen the size of my fist, and, for 30 lira for both of us, practically nothing, a mattress to crash on a rooftop filled with music, people and laughter.

We could have seen the sights the next day, but Rob wanted to hang out round the Pudding Club scene in Sultanahmet and I was loving every minute of what was happening.

And then we saw Lally. We watched as she made her way into the Pudding Club, and sat down at a table next to ours. By the time she'd ordered a drink, she and Rob were smiling, and by the time she'd finished it, they were sitting next to each other. That night I palled up with Clem, a guy from Bradford who'd been on our bus. It was his second time. He took me to a raki bar and we watched belly dancers.

'I've come to see the world,' he slurred. 'Not a bunch of hippies.' We nearly got run over by a taxi driver on the way back. Not my idea of fun.

Rob was besotted with Lally. She took him out, their first day together, and brought him back clad in ragged Ottoman finery to match her own. They danced on the rooftop, walked hand in hand, giggled endlessly, heads together, her white-blonde hair against his dark locks. Whatever he'd been looking for, he'd found it. His world exploded into colour now she was there. His feet barely touched the ground. He was euphoric, high on life, and love, and the golden girl who'd walked out of the sun.

And drugs. Not just hash, either. It only took a couple of nights on the rooftop to realise Lally was more intent on chemical flight than real-time journeying, and although she looked like an angel, she had the constitution of a horse as she smoked, downed pills, took whatever was on offer. 'I want to get out there,' she said, looking at Rob in awe. 'Right out there. Where you've been.'

They were inseparable. We missed our connection to Iran because Rob couldn't bear to leave her behind in Istanbul. 'A few more days, Ju-Ju-man,' he promised. 'Then we'll all go out together.' I was tempted to move on with Clem, but I'd promised to stay with Rob. I was happy enough, anyway. Life was cheap, and the living, on the Sultanahmet scene, was easy. The days slid by in a daze, and I barely noticed them passing.

When Rob came round on his rooftop mattress to find she'd done a moonlight flit, he flipped. 'She left a note. She said it had been a trip, and she hoped we'd meet along the road,' he ranted, shaking and crying, to me and anyone who would listen. But the freaks didn't like it when one of them lost their cool, and one by one the Pudding Club crowd shunned him.

'Time for him to move on,' someone advised me as he sat at a table on his own, shredding napkins, his jittery anxiety a force-field round him that kept everyone at arm's length. 'Get him out of here.'

I wished Clem was still around as I tried to rearrange our tickets and keep my brother from unravelling. Then he heard on the grapevine she'd gone to Afghanistan with a heavy Dutch crowd who could hook her up with some good connections. 'Kabul,' he told me. 'She talked about Kabul. We need to head for Kabul.' The thought of getting there, and finding her, filled him with frantic purpose.

Once we were on the bus, he calmed down a bit, though he wasn't interested in checking out anything en route. He slept on the bus, and the only thing he was bothered about was getting to Kabul. The nearer we got to Afghanistan, the more he seemed to level out. He even apologised for all the fuss he'd caused. 'I'm sorry Ju-Ju-man. We'll make it up to you, me and Lally, once we're in Kabul.' He'd convinced himself that all he needed to do was get there, and she'd be waiting for him. 'I understand it now,' he told me, somewhere out on the plains of Iran. With the endless unchanging horizon, time seemed to have ground to a halt. 'It's like a knight's quest in honour of his true lady. To prove his love.'

She wasn't there. With increasing desperation, we combed everywhere round Chicken Street. Every carpet shop, every tea shop, every guesthouse and hotel. No-one had seen her, or even heard of her. It got so that Rob was accosting strangers in the street, demanding if they knew of her. But no-one did.

Rob made less and less sense as the Kabul days went by and we didn't find her: either muttering and preoccupied or disjointedly restless. He gave off a scrambled nervous energy that made it hard to be with him. But I wasn't expecting the meltdown, where he didn't recognise me and fell to his knees in the courtyard at Siggy's and started banging his head on the floor, making sounds like an animal in pain, or how he lashed out when I went to help him up, and sent me flying. The Pashtun usually left the longhaired Inglistanis to their own devices, but this was disturbing their peace as well as everyone else's.

He was struggling so hard it took three of them to remove him. They pushed him in a room and locked the door. He banged and banged, and howled, and with tears in my eyes – and cash in my hands – I begged them to let him out. Or me in. 'Tomorrow you leave this place.' I nodded. I was shoved through the door, and once inside, I heard it being locked.

Shut up in that room with Rob was the most hellish night of my life, but only the beginning of the nightmare. When the Pashtun unlocked the door the next morning, and I emerged covered in bruises and scratches, I knew what my task must be. To get my brother out of there. To take him home.

There were no coaches due for days. It took nearly every penny I had but I bribed a driver to take us to the border where we could pick up a returning bus.

I tracked down a German who sold me a bottle of Temazepam. I sent a telegram back to Pinner. And somehow, just before the Temazepam ran out, I got Rob, the antique Ottoman finery Lally had found hanging off him in tatters, back home.

When Rob got out of hospital, he went to live with our parents. The medication kept him stable, though he put on quite a lot of weight. Mother took care of him, mostly. Dad couldn't cope with the way he didn't talk, even if you asked him a direct question, but he had his own key, and came and went, bicycling every day between Pinner Green and Hatch End, and as long as he never ran out of yellow paint, he was OK. He always painted the same thing, over and over again. A golden girl, walking out the sun.

Dad died in 1998, then Rob, in 2002. He had heart attack when he was out on his bicycle. He went straight away. Mother was nearly 80 by then, and looking after him had become more and more difficult for her, though when I offered to pay for help, she wasn't having any of it. She never said a word, but I think she blamed me for what happened.

I went back to Istanbul last year. After my divorce, I'd met a new partner, Wendy, and she'd always wanted to see the Blue Mosque. I'd had my doubts, though I kept them to myself, not wanting to spoil it for her, but it was stunning, and so were the other sights: Topkapi Palace, the Aya Sophia, the Bosphorus. 'I can't believe you never saw them before,' said Wendy, and I made her laugh by poking

fun at my younger self, hanging round with the other hairies instead of exploring when I was supposed to be on this great voyage of enlightenment.

I didn't tell her about Rob. He passed away long before I met Wendy, and there seemed no point in dredging up traumas from nearly four decades earlier. But one afternoon, I left her and another woman from our trip to go shopping in the Grand Bazaar, and I walked up to where I remembered the Pudding Shop. It was still there, so I went inside.

The freaks had long gone, though there were pictures and newspaper cuttings in a glass case on the wall. It was a self-service cafeteria now, so I chose a plate of rice and stewed peppers, and sat down. It was hard to imagine that this drab, functional place had once been the gateway where the colourful caravans of exotics had started their journey east.

It was only when I paid that I noticed the name on the bill. 'Lale,' it read. 'The famous Pudding Shop.'

And it struck me. The golden girl who walked out of the sun was just a kid who had named herself after a restaurant. Everyone in those days was looking for something. My brother found it. Perhaps she did, too.

KISSING TOADS

'I keep kissing them, but they always turn into toads!' bewailed Bettina. 'Princes keep on coming and coming, but they're never what they seem to be. At this rate, I'll end up an old maid and think I've had a lucky escape!' She flung herself on the sofa and prepared to go into hysterics.

'Get up immediately,' ordered The Fairy Godmother. 'Or your make-up will run and then nobody at all will want to kiss you. Stop sniveling. It doesn't suit you. You need to get a few things straight.'

Bettina looked up from the musty velvet depths of the sofa. The Fairy Godmother was an astringent old bird and her visits were a rare treat. Bettina had

been under her spell since she was a child, when the Fairy Godmother had let her into the kitchen to make witches' potions with food colouring. She also let her rootle around in any powder-scented drawers and fusty old jewellery boxes that took her fancy. Once, she'd shown her a particularly magical trick with a box shaped like a tortoise. When smoke exhaled from its wooden mouth without anyone so much as lighting a cigarette, Bettina was convinced that the Fairy Godmother had special powers. Nothing had ever shaken this conviction.

If that hadn't been enough to make up her mind, there were autumn walks on the nearby green collecting crab-apples from beneath swirls of rusty, ice-encrusted fallen leaves to make into silver-sprayed Christmas centre-pieces; afternoons spent delving through boxes for forgotten treasures in the clanking Anderson shelter; mornings spent stroking the black cat Sunday who slept in a drawer in the dresser whilst the Godmother drank Guinness from a teacup and concocted recipes made with exotic spices which didn't come from the same shops Bettina's mother used, and whole late-summer days braving the brambles in the overgrown garden to collect plump berries which turned into dark and delicious jam. There were all the times when the Fairy Godmother had known exactly what Bettina wanted for her birthdays, without being asked. There was her smell: stout, dense musky old perfume, clothes made in long-forgotten styles from fabrics that changed colour in the light. And the way she always knew everything, ever, that you always wanted to know and never dared ask anyone else.

Aware that Bettina was in limbo between the safe past and the fraught present, the Fairy Godmother patted her black crepe knee. She believed in dressing for each day as if it were an occasion. Her clothes looked like nothing on earth, and no-one ever knew where she got them. 'What has happened? Or rather,' she said beadily. 'Who. Who has managed to make you so miserable?'

Bettina didn't need further prompting. She let her woes spill out and wash her in a deep flood of misery, and some sooty tears where her mascara ran. 'It's Josh,' she wailed. 'The good looking one.'

'They've all been good looking so far,' snapped the Fairy Godmother. 'At least, they have on the outside.'

Bettina ignored her. 'I've been seeing him for eight weeks and we were getting on really well. He was like a dream come true - a hero in a romantic novel. He swept me right off my feet and there was nothing I could do to stop it.'

'You're getting carried away,' said the Fairy Godmother. 'You sound like Barbara Cartland. We're talking about you and the marketing manager from a coffee chain, not Brad Pitt and Angelina Jolie.'

'It was just like that though,' snuffled Bettina through a fresh wave of Lancôme-lashed tears. 'It was different from anything that has ever happened to me before.'

'Humph,' snorted the Fairy Godmother.

Bettina ignored that, too.

'I know he could be moody, but that was part of his charm,' she intoned. Her eyes went all starry. 'He was unpredictable. If he smiled, it was as if the sun had broken out from behind a storm cloud. He made me feel as if I was the only person in the world who could make this happen.'

'So you were the miracle he'd been waiting for all his life?' queried the Fairy Godmother in neutral tones.

'Yes. Exactly that,' enthused Bettina.

'You've got very selective hearing,' mentioned the Fairy Godmother.

Bettina wailed. 'You just think this is funny! But my whole life is in ruins!'

'I know the sort you mean,' returned the Godmother. 'It's their way of keeping you on your toes. You're so desperately grateful when they do behave well that it makes up for all the times they've been unspeakable.'

'Have you met people like that too?' cooed a wide-eyed Bettina. 'I thought I was the only one.' The Godmother said nothing, but her pointed toe twitched in what might have been exasperation. Bettina didn't notice. She carried on with her tale of woe.

'Two nights ago, he collected me to go to a house party. When we got there, he threw himself headlong at the cocktails and a blonde in a bandage dress. She's called Samantha Bottomley. Then he disappeared for ages, and so did she. I found them both under the coats in one of the bedrooms. I had to get Todd to bring me home.'

'The Fairy Godmother nodded wisely. 'Sounds as if you're best off without him. Men like that are a complete waste of space. All surface and no substance. Now tell me about Todd.'

Bettina looked dismissive. 'Oh, him. He works in my office. He's been after me for ages but I wouldn't touch him with a bargepole. He's really sweet, but he just isn't the sort of man girls fancy.'

'Why not,' snapped the Godmother. 'What's wrong with him. Has he got two heads or something? And nothing in his underpants?'

'It's not like that,' huffed Bettina. 'He's just...Todd. He's good and sweet and kind, and he's always there when you need him. He wouldn't hurt a fly and you always know that, whatever you do, he won't turn against you. Like I said, he just isn't sexy. I know it's a shame, but there it is.'

'No accounting for taste, is there?' the Fairy Godmother asked nobody in particular. 'You mean he isn't as devilishly handsome as the smooth and superficial seducer Josh.' This fork-tongued remark was directed at the hapless Bettina, who didn't reply because her mind, hopping like a TV screen from channel to channel, was filled with an unwelcome vision of Todd sitting at his drawing board. Big, short-sighted eyes blinked at her from behind huge blue-rimmed glasses. His moon face was split from ear to ear in a toothy grin. Floppy red hair fell around his ears. A lurid shirt covered in dragons that looked as if it glowed in the dark covered his broad chest. There was a coating of red-brown hair visible where the top buttons had come undone. He wasn't, mused Bettina, a vision of male beauty.

Mentally she contrasted him with Josh. He was mean and moody, and his profile was magnificent. His burnished dark hair was slicked back from a high forehead. His smouldering eyes were deepest blue. He had a chin that might have been carved in granite. When he spoke, it was in a voice so seductive Bettina felt as if she was clad only in her underwear even if he was simply asking her to check an error on an Excel spreadsheet. A dreamy smile flickered over her face.

It changed swiftly into a pout, then a frown, as Samantha Bottomley sashayed into the frame, encased in something clinging and black which left nothing to the imagination. Her face wore the same expression as a cat whose not only got the cream, but knows there's a lot more of it on offer. An involuntary wail of misery escaped from Bettina'a forlorn pink lips, and another mascara-tear dripped onto her already damp bosom.

Seeing such a pathetic sight, the Fairy Godmother, who had wanted to say something sharp, decided to be kind instead. She stroked Bettina's soft blond curls, letting her cry for a moment. 'I know it's horrible my dear,' she consoled, 'but you must look

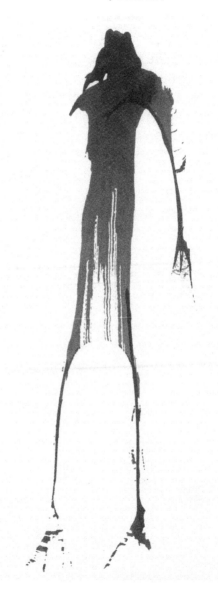

in your heart and decide what it is you really want in a man. That's the only way anything magical is ever going to happen. There's no such thing as chance in these affairs, you know.' Bettina snuffled. The Fairy Godmother carried on. 'It's amazing what can happen when you really look at people, instead of just seeing the pretty faces they wear in public.'

Bettina looked puzzled. 'I'm not sure,' she said dimly, 'exactly what you mean.'

The Godmother gave up. 'Before I go,' she said at last, with just a hint of exasperation, 'I'm going to give you a wish. It comes with a warning, because if you wish hard enough for what you think you want you will get it, which is not always a good thing. If you wish for what you need, no harm will come to you.' With that, she primped herself in a hand-mirror, took a swift nip from an elderly pewter hip-flask, arranged a moulting fur collar around her and left with much swishing and swirling of her umbrella, because it was raining outside.

Bettina sat on the sofa, wishing as hard as she could. So it might have been hours later, or only minutes, that her smartphone vibrated. When Bettina saw the name on her screen, a beatific smile suffused her tear-stained face.

'Of course it doesn't matter Josh!' she exclaimed. 'You're right. You're always right. It was just me, over-reacting. Yes, isn't it amazing what a bit too much drink can do? And you've known her for ages, of course you have. Yes, I know, I was only being stupid. Yes, of course you can. I'm so pleased to hear you, thank you for ringing. See you in a bit.'

She put the Samsung on the sofa and sat back down next to it. She'd got exactly what she'd wished for but it was funny, she didn't feel exactly... happy. Josh always made her feel like that. Small. Strained. A bit stupid. It was because he was so clever. She didn't know what she'd say to him when he arrived. Against her will, she acknowledged an image of Samantha Bottomley's expertly contoured face smiling victoriously at her over Josh's immaculately suited shoulder. Somehow they'd fitted together perfectly, like two pieces of an executive toy. Bettina shuddered. The Samsung vibrated again.

'Oh it's you Todd,' she said, flatly but trying not to be unkind. 'Yes honestly, I'm fine. I was just a bit under the weather. I'll be back in tomorrow, I'm OK. Really.' She put the receiver down again. Kind old Todd, he always made so much fuss. He'd make someone a lovely husband.

Bettina sat up straight. She hadn't meant to think that at all.

The rain was dashing down so hard that Bettina only faintly heard the sound of a car outside. But as

its door slammed, she rushed to the front door and flung it wide open.

Outside the air was speckled so silver with the pelting rain that Bettina

could hardly make out a thing. But she saw that as each great drop landed on the gravel stones in the drive, a miniscule, almost transparent frog bounced into the air. She watched, entranced, as the ground became a speckled, shimmering mass of tiny, jumping baby frogs and luminous drops of shifting rainbow-coloured water. For the first time that day her small, worried face relaxed into a smile of unadulterated happiness.

She was so busy watching the minute, leaping amphibians cavorting in the fast-moving deluge that it took her moments to realise Todd was standing at the end of the drive, soaked to the skin, with an armful of flowers and an expression which made his eyes shine behind the water-logged blue goggles. As she watched, the clouds parted to let the sun through. Its rays illuminated the raindrops so they looked like multi-faceted diamonds of light shining all round Todd's head. He was looking directly into her eyes as a huge rainbow wrapped itself round the whole scene like a giant ribbon and took Bettina's breath away with its beauty.

Treading with great care so as not to crush a single tiny one of them, Bettina picked her way though the silvery dancing frogs to go into Todd's arms. The flowers fell on the floor but she didn't care. She felt safe for the first time ever.

'You sounded so sad on the phone,' he said, 'that I thought I'd better come and see if you were all right.'

Bettina looked at Todd, and saw, because it seemed the right thing to do, that underneath his orange hair and huge spectacles, his face was strong and gentle and almost handsome. His big round eyes were glowing with love. Bettina wanted to stay in his arms, in the pouring rain, for ever and ever.

When Josh pulled up in his sleek black BMW minutes later, the first thing he saw was Bettina and Todd. They were kissing in the downpour and thousands of tiny frogs were playing in the raindrops all around them. And he noticed the air was perfumed, faintly but quite distinctly, with a scent reminiscent of Guinness, musty, old-fashioned perfume and the secret places in the backs of ancient wardrobes.

INTO THE BLUE

When Eric first heard his diagnosis he didn't wash or take his clothes off for four days. He couldn't face confronting his reflection in the mirror or the sight of his naked flesh because of the thing he knew his body harboured. For four days, fear made him unable to look at the surface of himself, and his hands, feet and fingers went numb. Then he stopped feeling anything inside.

'I know I'm going to die,' he said without a hint of melodrama. 'That's what it's like. It's like nothing. No light at the end of the tunnel. I'm a speck. A particle. A great big heap of nothing.' But he was so numb he didn't care.

When the feeling came back, it was like an intense flood. It transfixed him in a way he hadn't known to be possible, and it took him a lot of puzzled consideration to work out what it was. He looked in the mirror for significant changes that might account for it, but there was nothing he could pinpoint with the naked eye. He looked in his fridge to see what he'd been eating which might have made a difference; not that there was much to choose from. Nothing sprang to mind. But to his immense surprise, he realised the feeling was love, and it flowed from him with such clarity and abundance he gradually became surrounded by a visible aura.

The feeling was peculiar: a prickly tension between his skin and the air, which made him particularly aware of his body's energies. He could feel something emanating from him but it was intangible, although he could sense it stopped some four inches away from his skin. The outer edges of his aura tingled with a strange electricity that made him feel as though he were being continually caressed by the tips of a lover's fingers. But it wasn't a sexual feeling.

'Ooh,' he smiled to himself, concentrating hard. 'This is nice. I like this.' He realised it was the first time he'd really liked anything without being chemically enhanced since he was seventeen, when he'd been taken to Brighton for a day-trip. He'd spent the day sitting under the pier, watching the water lapping upon the pebbles and a band of twelve year old nutters throwing themselves from the girders into the murky sea. But that was a long time ago.

The new aura moved in response to every motion his body made. When he looked in the mirror he could see it clearly, glowing round him. He'd never thought he was especially nice to look at, especially not without a good wash and brush up and some expensive odds and ends of slap, but when the blue glow cast silvery lights across his pale, skinny body, he began to think he wasn't so bad after all. In a strange but comforting way, he noticed that on days he felt particularly ill, the aura got brighter. And oddly, warmer, as if it were wrapping itself round him like a comforting cosmic blanket.

'That's the thermals in the bin for starters,' he decided. 'No point looking like a tramp on your deathbed. You never know who might be looking.'

The aura wasn't something he could hide under clothing. No matter how many layers he piled on, it shone through with a stubborn refusal to be extinguished. Eric got used to his aura, and then liked it, but found it rather embarrassing walking round on his daily business, surrounded by a halo of bright blue light. He was convinced that strangers were pointing at him behind his back, sniggering as though he'd forgotten to dress himself properly. 'What are you looking at?' he'd taunt them. 'Haven't you ever seen one like this before?'

His illness had made him self-conscious. It was too new for him not to feel that people could see the sickness written on him. If anyone he didn't know looked too hard, he was convinced they knew what was wrong with him. He didn't understand the feeling. Gradually, though, the aura began to help him. He began to understand that it was a visible manifestation of all the love he'd stored up during his lifetime, but never given himself a chance to spend. When he thought about it, he saw that he'd spent his time holding himself back from other people, treating them like insurance policies, waiting to see what was the best deal he could get out of them. But now, his aura gave him a magical warmth which let off so much other heat he couldn't help spreading it around.

Other people warmed to it, too. They so rarely came across unconditional love and unconditional acceptance that Eric found himself with almost more friends than he knew what to do with. 'I'll have to start giving them tickets,' he thought. 'Like they do in the supermarket.'

The more he got used to it, the more he found there were positive advantages to having an aura that insisted on being noticed. In clubs, Eric was particularly sought after because it of its spectacular fluorescent glow, which showed to great effect under the UV lighting. A photographer was found who dealt in special effects, and pictures of a rail-thin, spectacularly smiling Eric adorned a million lifestyle web pages. 'That's me, that is. Doesn't she look lovely,' he grinned. 'Well I would say that, wouldn't I?' The look trended on Twitter with the hashtag #bluelight, and cosmetic manufacturers worked day and night to produce a cream which would replicate his trademark blue glow. It cost a lot of money despite the barely-there packaging, but it sold like hot cakes from the kind of chi-chi cosmetics emporiums that have queues outside.

Despite the debilitating effects of his illness, Eric discovered his limbs could move with a new lightness. Before, his dancing had been nothing special, but now he was able to move with a winning fluidity that drew all eyes in his direction. He was on the guest list of every club in the country. 'I can't be everywhere at once you know,' he tutted. But he was pleased with the attention all the same. Offers to accompany him home got to be something of an embarrassment because although he didn't want to hurt the feelings of anybody who asked, he simply couldn't find time for everybody.

Although he was open-minded, even positive, about the changes he was undergoing, the discovery of nodules growing on his hitherto smooth shoulders was a terrible shock. On each side of his neck he felt a hard, pulsating bump, which was tender to the touch rather than actually painful. In front of his bathroom mirror, Eric examined the swellings with anxious fingers. They weren't the first manifestation of his physical state but they were the most alarming and he didn't think it would be long before they started to hurt. He went to bed with a hot-water bottle, hoping that an early night and a good sleep would mean he felt better in the morning.

When he awoke the next morning, he felt two heavy weights dragging his body backwards onto the mattress. Putting his hand up to investigate the state of the lumps, he encountered a soft, fluffy mass of feathers. Startled awake, he twisted his head to one side, and discovered he was the owner of two brand new, beautifully plumed white wings.

'Bugger me sideways with a lamp-post,' was the only thing he could think of to say.

Leaping out of bed to examine them further, he realised they were gorgeous.

'Ooh lovely,' he preened. 'Very nice indeed.'

Reaching to the floor on either side of him, they fluttered gently. When he moved, they flowed in accordance with whatever his body did. Suddenly elated, he pulled up his trance playlist on Spotify. As uplifting repetitive beats filled the air, Eric

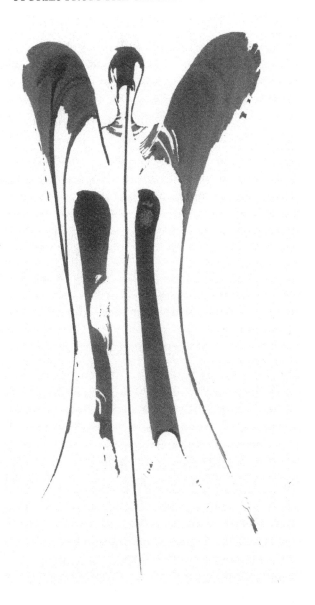

danced ecstatically round his bedroom, feeling the wondrous wings lifting him so that he hovered above the carpet, suspended in the air as he danced, filled with an overwhelming joy.

'This is it,' he realised. 'I can die happy now. Whatever happens I've had my own miracle.' The pain magically flowed from his limbs, his head, his torso. The blotches on his skin seemed to fade. And the ball of confusion which had been buried deep in his stomach shrank to the size of a pea. His smile went from one side of his face to the other. 'Give over,' he grinned. 'You great big fairy.' If he'd had a wand, he'd have waved it all over the world, sparkling spangled dust over friends, enemies and complete strangers. But as he was alone, he let the waves of ecstasy wash over him. All of him. It was all for him.

He stayed at home the whole day, testing his wings and getting to know them. When he had a rest, they curled up round him to keep him warm. When he wanted to cook food, they tucked themselves neatly behind him, out of his way. 'Nice manners,' he whispered as he stroked them approvingly. Although they were quite heavy, when they were in motion they seemed to weigh nothing. When they lifted him off the ground – which happened frequently and involuntarily – the sensation of weighing nothing was transferred to Eric's own slight body.

In the evening, Eric noticed his wings becoming restless, rather like limbs that wanted to be stretched.

It crossed his mind that they wanted to be exercised. 'Go on, have a good flap,' he suggested, standing in the middle of the living room. Obligingly, the heavy wings wriggled and shook. Eric couldn't quite manage to stand still while they did it, and he ended up arse over on the carpet. The wings kindly lifted him back on his feet, and the tip of the left one stroked him solicitously to make sure nothing was hurt. His skin looked as if it had been brushed with gold flakes where the wing touched it.

Eric realised he hadn't worn clothing all day. Even if he'd wanted to, arranging the wings inside jeans and a shirt would have been like wearing a sweatshirt tucked into pants, only more insulting. He looked down at his bare body and saw that the blue aura was darker than ever, highlighted by traces of gold where the wing tip had brushed against flesh. As he pondered about the Pharaoh's combination of bright blue and dark gold he now sported instead of the usual flaky pink and blotchy, the wings ruffled and stretched up behind him. His feet lifted a few inches off the carpet and his heart leapt almost into his mouth. It was a rush like none he'd ever experienced before.

As he tried to stay earthed, the wings pushed him towards the window. He was too taken aback to do more than try and drag his heels on the ground. 'Stoppit!' he squawked. 'Give over!' The wings took no notice. The window was open and Eric could feel his heart in his mouth as the wings swooped him off his feet in one easy lift, straight through the narrow space. He screwed his eyes shut and mustered up the strength to scream, but was overwhelmed by the worst coming-up nausea he'd ever felt. Then it stopped. He opened his eyes a bit, to find he was suspended calmly in mid-air, totally still, held up by the great wings fluttering gently as he got his breath back. 'I get vertigo,' he said to himself. 'I'm scared of heights.' But as he hung in mid-air with more serenity than he'd ever known he could muster, he wasn't.

It was only a moment between standing upright and embarking on his first solo flight. But it changed him forever. After the initial shock of finding he was gliding past clouds rather than plummeting through them, the sheer exhilaration of flight took over. Eric gave himself up to a mindless, wordless sense of union with time and space as he soared through the sky. Below him, pinpricks of light joined to form a spangling snake of colour which coiled its way round streets and houses like an endless, gleaming, multi-coloured serpent with a thousand heads and a million tails. Currents of air made his body bob and dip, but the strong outstretched pinions seemed to know instinctively how to navigate in strong, straight lines. They beat only occasionally, conserving their force, riding the night sky with calm and might. Eric was most surprised at how natural it all felt. 'I was born for this,' he exulted. 'This is who I was meant to be.'

His debut solo flight took him over territory that was familiar, but, from this new perspective, totally alien. He saw the tiny bodies of his friends disappearing into the subterranean warren of the nightlife world. He passed over houses whose interiors he knew intimately and wondered what their inhabitants would think to know that he was passing directly overhead, and could see into their windows. He had a strong temptation to shout 'Cooeee! Only me! I know what you're up to!' but decided it would be inappropriate. Naked and bewinged, he felt less of a night life trollop and more like an elemental, mythic creature who had been granted the rare possibility of seeing the world in a way totally inaccessible to humankind. Yet there was no pride in his feelings; only awe. He knew he was being taken care of in a way that was beyond his wildest dreams.

Finally, the great wings turned him around and took him back to his own flat. Although the open window was a tiny target, he was flown gently into an immaculately smooth landing, feet squarely on the carpet. The feathered limbs rustled, then shivered slightly and settled themselves comfortably round him. He was exhausted, and dropped into bed like a log. Falling instantly into a deep doze, he slept in the soft embrace of the wings, which gathered him into their depths so he had no need of the duvet. His last waking thought was 'Wow.'

Whilst Eric slept, four white, winged creatures flew silently in through the open window, and stood around his bed. The wings rustled to acknowledge the visitors' presence, but his body was still. The creatures bought a strange bright light into the room; under its effect, Eric's aura expanded into fluorescent haze, which filled the room with luminous blue. There was no sound, no sound at all.

For a long while, the angels remained in their places bathed in blue light, but when the first dawn haze began to creep across the dark night skyline, they bent over Eric's reclining form. There weren't any words spoken, but their thoughts seemed to say: 'It's time now, for you to come with us.' They extended their hands to Eric, who rose into the light and held out his hands. Behind him, the wings rose into the blue air. A beatific smile lit his face; as he moved towards the window in the company of the angels who flanked him so he didn't feel lonely, his feet glided like theirs, six inches above the carpet. The five winged beings moved in unison towards the window.

As dawn broke, if anybody had been coming home from a night on the tiles and looked upwards to see five joyous white winged forms flying higher and higher above the clouds, they wouldn't have been dreaming, or hallucinating, or imagining things. They'd have seen Eric in the company of angels, leaving behind a world of sorrow, and sickness, and pain.

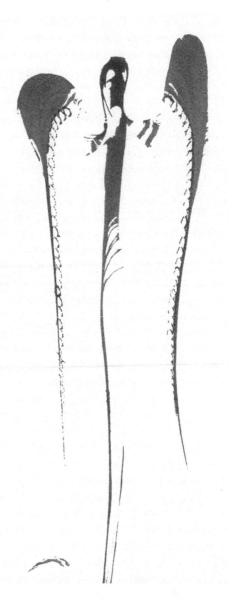

TEMPEST AND THE GHOST

Tempest sat on the stool in the kitchen waiting for the ghost to come out of the airing cupboard. He sat like that every night. He knew she was in there. He could feel her presence all over the flat. Several times he'd almost seen her, out of the corner of his eye.

Tempest wasn't the only one who knew the flat was haunted. Maria had once seen her, an eighteenth-century servant, dressed in black, disappearing into the wall. Julie had glimpsed her hovering in a corner. Jane had stayed awake all night, convinced the ghost was in the room with her. Carmen co-existed with her happily for years, and in return, the ghost always made sure the flat welcomed her warmly whenever she came home.

When she lived in the flat, Penny saw the ghost every night at midnight, when she would walk across the living room. Penny's round brown eyes would follow her progress, and the hairs down her spine would stand on end when the ghost passed silently on her nightly round as she inspected that all was well before retiring for the night. And Penny would bolt her dinner in the kitchen, where the ghost lived, but never sit in there when she was relaxing, or go in there unless there was a very good reason. But Penny was a Jack Russell, and beyond tracking the ghost's progress with a low 'wuff... wuff... wuff,' she couldn't make anyone understand exactly what it was she could see.

The flat was part of a very old hall, built over the passage of time into a warren of chambers and passages. It wasn't surprising that a ghostly presence had been caught between time zones, as one builder after another had trapped slices of atmosphere between the walls of his construction. Or maybe the presence was so attached to the place that it had decided to linger, making sure everything was maintained to the standards the ghost had set when she was flesh and blood, not a hint, or a memory, or an impression of herself.

Tempest found himself ensconced in the flat after walking out of his old life. He was formerly a legendary cabaret creation: a celebrity chanteuse and divine dancer of the most fabulous gender-ambiguous nightclub ever to coat its walls as thickly in ambience as in red-flock wallpaper and spangles. She arrived from the east after dancing her way through floorshows and boudoirs in exotic nightspots and intercontinental fleshpots where the who and the what of a person were defined by careful strokes of the brush in a make-up mirror, by dresses made by hand because no pattern could ever be sufficiently lavish to accommodate the wealth of her imagination, where male body became female flesh in the time it took to shiver into fishnets, slide into satin and glue a set of spidery eyelashes above eyes wide open to any possibilities.

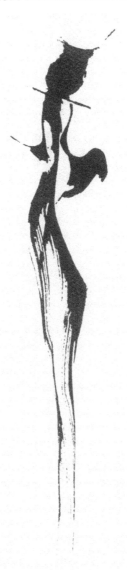

Tempest was the icy blonde beauty with the rhinestone eye patch who made Marlene Dietrich look kitten-friendly by comparison, the slinky mover in bias-cut lilac with the razor-edged repartee which could kill at 100 paces, the long-limbed limelight-dweller who, with biology-defying languor, could kick in slow motion so high into the air that one slim mesh-clad thigh would reside parallel to a cheekbone which could cut paper. She was a star, out of the orbit of ordinary showgirls, even ones with penises. As if to prove it, she left a trail of glitter, or a sequin, or even the odd rhinestone, wherever she went.

Of course it couldn't last. The management of the fabulous nightspot spent more time hoovering in the toilets than laundering the bills. The girls were so badly paid and so over-worked that many of them used the cabaret as a display for other, more personal services. For the punters, it was a haven of miraculous ambiguity. For the workers, it was an unrelenting nightmare. Pumped full of off-prescription drugs on a 24-hour cycle, more highly strung than an aerial trapeze artist and as utterly dedicated to ensuring everything that was supposed to happen, did, Tempest made dresses, designed routines, rehearsed the troupe, performed every night and made sure the place didn't fall apart. It was the only thing that held her together.

Then the fragile structure stretched to breaking point. Tempest stalked onto the stage one night and saw the manager and his cronies, noses powdered, smirking at their usual table at the thought of the immense profits rolling their way through the day-in-day-out efforts of Tempest and the girls. She imagined them like dogs, with long tongues that lapped at their coke-filled noses, with raw red dog-cocks, which they would later try to rub up on the legs of showgirls to whom they barely paid a living wage. The stimulants making her blood race acted like a truth drug. She prowled to the front of the stage in her spike shoes, wielding the microphone like a weapon. 'The manager's over there,' she drawled to the punters, pointing at him with laser directness. 'He sucks cocks if you ask him nicely.' In the silence that followed, every tap tap tap of her heels reverberated like a time bomb. 'And those drinks you're holding...' she continued, knowing there was no turning back. She didn't want there to be. 'Sip them. They're already watered down, and the mark-up's 400%.'

She'd launched a rocket. She was fired. Then she crashed. And burned. Then she went to live by the sea for a long time, watching the waves and sitting in the sun until her skin was dark golden. And in a while the overwhelmingness of ordinary life became easier to handle, and she realised she wanted to come back home, and for some things never to be as they were again. She grew a finely contoured Van Dyck beard and returned to England, commissioned by a friend to make alien creatures from another galaxy to inhabit a strange night-club world. It was only a variation on what she'd done all her life.

Tempest left the old dresses in a suitcase and forgot where it was, referred to himself as 'he' again, and came to stay in the flat where the ghost lived in the airing cupboard. 'You will leave me some nice bits of drag,' he said hopefully, as he arranged with the owner about getting the keys.

At first Tempest knew the ghost was there because he'd been told about her. He rather looked forward, in a slightly apprehensive way, to living somewhere haunted. And he could feel the flat felt warmly about him. But the first night he slept there, although it felt welcoming, he could sense her. He slept with the light on, waking up to peer into the shadows. He tried to frighten himself with the thought that she was there, but somehow felt strangely safe.

The ghost stood silently in the corner of the room. She watched while Tempest fell asleep despite the nightlight. She smiled softly at him, and approached the bed. She patted the duvet with a steady, gentle hand. There was a faint trace of gilded glitter, which she dabbed with a finger. Over the years she'd understood that things were different from what they'd been when she was alive. She could see that the duvet was similar to the old feather quilts she'd shaken out daily, hundreds of years ago. Tempest stirred slightly and the ghost reached out a finger to touch the very tip of one of his golden curls. Then she glided back to the shadows in the corner.

As days passed, Tempest tried hard to see the form of the ghost he could feel was never far away from him. His glasses were a state, the lenses covered in grease and the frame with one missing leg. He constructed a makeshift elastic band to hold them onto his face, and peered hard at the airing cupboard. No ghost. Disgusted, he left the glasses on the kitchen sideboard and sat on the sequin-scattered sofa, smoking cigarettes with his elegant long fingers, and designing costumes he might want to wear in the future.

The ghost looked round the empty kitchen. 'No wonder he can't see anything,' she thought. 'Those eyeglasses need a good polish.' She picked up a clean dishcloth and breathed heavily on the dirty lenses. 'Men,' she thought. 'They never clean anything properly.'

Tempest thought he must have absent-mindedly polished the disreputable spectacles when he picked them up the next day. He went out to work as usual. When he came home from work at midnight, he'd had a line of speed much earlier and it hadn't worn off. He climbed into a pair of Vivienne Westwood platforms and was seized with a fit of cleaning frenzy. He hoovered the carpets, polished the sideboard and washed the kitchen floor at three in the morning. The ghost stood by, delighted to have her preconceptions altered. 'Well I never,' she said to herself. 'Things have changed.' When Tempest finally collapsed into bed, exhausted, the ghost perched on the edge of the bed, solicitous and slightly worried. 'He'll wear himself out,' she thought. 'If he carries on like this.' The next day was a Sunday, and Tempest had a day off. He spent most of it asleep, curled up in bed, and the ghost stayed in his room to make sure he was all right. Tempest, in a half-sleep, mused on the fact that he didn't feel alone even though he was the only person in the flat. He had lovely dreams, too.

After that, the ghost kept an eye on him. When he lost the credit card bill he needed to pay, she put it where he'd find it before he got into trouble for not keeping up with his payments. When he thought he'd forgotten to switch the washing machine on, he came back to find the wash had been done. And the ghost kindly turned down the cooker so that a pan didn't boil over when Tempest was having a very long phone conversation with his friend Belle in Manchester.

The ghost also watched, with absorbed interest, as Tempest fitted up his sewing machine in the living room and began to make ridiculously beautiful garments out of pieces of fabric he picked up cheap in the market, and patterns he made up in his head. And she was amazed when he modelled them with a dancer's grace and the incredible style which had made him the star of any show he was ever in. It had always been the ghost's ambition to be a lady's maid. She was star-struck. When he wasn't there, she unfolded the material he was working with, and held it wonderingly against herself. Tempest sometimes noticed that the fabric wasn't folded quite as he'd left it. He wondered about this as he sat on the kitchen stool, gazing at the airing cupboard. He knew she was in there.

The last day of making aliens was finished off for Tempest with a giant spliff, which the giver had forgotten to mention was packed with industrial-strength skunk. It blew the top of Tempest's head off, and left him feeling totally paranoid and incapable of any other function except drooling. 'I will go and sit in the bath,' he thought woodenly. 'And get clean. That will sort me out. Then I must go and pack the aliens in the van so they can be taken to London. I have got to do this or I will let people down.'

He filled the bath with hot water and sat in it. 'I must wash myself,' he thought. 'I am dirty.' The water was warm and it was nice and what was left of Tempest's brain after the spliff shut even further down. He tried to work out which was water and which was him, but couldn't tell the difference. 'I must wash myself,' insisted a small voice at the back of his brain. But his arms and brain didn't function in connection with each other. Tempest wallowed in the bath and wondered about the way he seemed to have become one with the bath water. 'I must wash myself,' said the small voice distantly. 'I am dirty.'

A bath sponge hit him in the face. The exasperated ghost had thrown it at him. 'Frame yourself you great lump,' said the ghost, although Tempest couldn't hear her. 'Don't just sit there in your own dirt, wash yourself.' Tempest came to with a bump. The sponge had been on a shelf at the other end of the bathroom. Now it was in the bath, and it had not got there by itself. He gave himself a good scrub and shot out of the water and into his clothes like a rat up a drainpipe. Later, when his brain was working properly, and he was in a van half-way to London, he realised what had happened. 'I don't believe it,' he told himself. Then, 'Jesus.'

He was away for a week. The ghost took advantage of his absence. The bath episode had made her feel quite brave. At first, she held his dresses against herself. Then she slid one on. Tempest was six foot tall, and the slinky skirt had been made to accommodate seven-inch heels. It was far too long for her; she held it up with both hands. It was the most gorgeous thing she had ever seen. She looked in the mirror. The dress appeared animated in the glass. She moved a step or two, and the dress moved with her. She picked up a handful of skirt, and dropped a curtsey. The dress bobbed gracefully in the mirror. The ghost tilted her head admiringly, this way and that, but she couldn't see any reflection of herself whatsoever.

The next day, she tried on another one. It was midnight blue and silver, even more fabulous than the first. She danced to a tune she remembered from hundreds of years ago, stumbling at first, with steps she hadn't executed for centuries, round the living room floor. She sat on the sofa, mimicking the way Tempest sat, although her short legs didn't achieve quite the same effect as his long ones. She caressed the velvet material in sweeping strokes, and wondered at her own impudence. She'd never worn anything apart from her stuff outfit, black and grey, since she went into service over two hundred years ago.

Each day it was the same. Almost reverently, she tried on one of Tempest's creations over her own clothes, and danced around the flat. She had never been so happy before.

When Tempest walked through the door, he got the shock of his life. One of his dresses was frisking round the living room all by itself. Tempest, rooted to the spot, was so scared he thought he was going to have a heart attack. The ghost froze in horror, and then backed away.

Although he could hardly think for terror, Tempest realised the ghost was even more mortified than he was. He took a very deep breath, and walked towards the CD player.

'Shall we have some music?' he asked the thin air. 'You look gorgeous.' He selected an old tune with a languorous waltz tempo, and gracefully approached the ghost. 'Would you like to dance?' he asked, very politely.

The ghost was enchanted. No-one had ever asked her before. Quivering, she placed her little hand in Tempest's, although he felt nothing. He put his hand lightly on the back of his dress, and was amazed when it moved in response to his touch. But all those years of show business had taught him that, even under the strangest circumstances, the show must go on. Carefully and precisely, he began to dance the ghost round and round, leading her so expertly she didn't realise she wasn't moving all by

herself, twirling her into perfect shapes, whisking her through steps which were too complicated for her to remember afterwards.

She was ecstatic. When the dance came to an end, if Tempest had been able to see her, he would have recognised a radiant smile adorning a face flushed with happiness. He bowed gallantly. 'Do you mind,' he asked, 'if I have my dress back?'

The ghost slid it from her shoulders. It dropped to the floor with a velvet whisper. Then the ghost, being braver than she'd ever been when she was alive, put her small hands into Tempest's, and kissed him very gently on the cheek. 'Thank you,' she whispered. Tempest realised later that he had heard her say it.

Later, he sat on the stool in the kitchen, looking at the airing cupboard where she lived. He could almost see her, out of the corner of his eye. He knew she was there. There was a faint sprinkling of golden glitter, about five feet from the ground, where her cheek had, just for a split second, brushed against his.

EVERYTHING HAS ITS PLACE

Gold is not always worth what it seems. But once upon a time it seemed worth everything. It seemed worth a life.

I have learned my lesson. Even though it glitters, gold is a base metal.

My hair is not golden any more, and my once golden skin is now the colour of sour buttermilk, and it fits less well than it once did. But for all that, I am still a queen. Once upon a time, my golden looks – and my golden touch – earned me a crown.

You have to understand – where I come from, families went hungry. When the crops failed, we had to live on our wits. We were always looking for an opportunity because it meant putting food on the table. To us, a full belly was riches.

But I possessed a different kind of riches – golden skin, golden hair. I looked as if honey ran in my veins, and the sun shone from inside me.

My father the miller knew I was worth more than money in the bank, so to keep that lush, well-fed glow, I was fed the best of everything we had, and any spare money was spent on adorning me. I was clad in soft linen, but my brothers and sisters made do with rags, and howled when I was given milk and they had to make do with filling their empty bellies with water. No wonder I thought so much of myself. I was brought up to believe that my looks made me a treasure.

Hardship makes people hard. My father understood that he would need to work hard to get the best return from his investment. And like a gambler, to place all his cards on the table when it looked as if the jackpot was in sight. When the king came to our village, he knew that this was the best chance he would get to trade the hard grind for a life of comfort.

Everyone knew that the king was a collector, and a miser, and a snob. He loved beautiful things. He loved to hide them away, and gloat over their value. He would never marry a barefoot girl from the villages, no matter how bright her beauty might shine. But what if…

My father let it be known – cursed be the day the thought first crossed his mind – that his golden daughter had an exceptional gift: that when she spun straw it would turn to gold.

What could make me more irresistible? The king looked on my face, and the butter-toned skin that swelled gently over my bodice, and he rubbed himself in that most private of gentlemen's places. His purse.

'I can't do it.'

'You have to do it. I have given my word.'

I was locked in a room, with a spindle and a bale of straw. And the fear.

Can you imagine?

You know the rest of the story. They say that once upon a time, the strange little man came, three nights running, and how, each following morning, the room was filled with gold instead of straw. Three days running, they say, the king looked at me, and he looked at the gold, and he wanted more. Three nights running, the little man came. They say I gave him first my necklace, then my ring, and then when I had no more to give, I promised him my first-born child. They say that when the child was born, and the little man came for him, and insisted that unless I discovered his name, the child was his, I had the country scoured to find what the strange little man was called. And the story goes that when I said the name aloud the strange little man was so maddened that he plunged his leg down all the way into the bowels of the earth, and tore himself in two.

My husband, the king, tired of me long before my beauty faded, but I am, after all, a queen. So he could not cast me aside, but although I am tended with all ceremony, my apartments are far from his. It's a lonely life. The servant girls will not gossip with me and my aristocratic attendants sneer at me behind my back, because I am low-born. My husband never visits me.

And so I am left alone with my thoughts, and as I grow older, they often return to the strange little man, and the three nights we shared. Something magical happened on each of those nights, and it left a golden glow in the air, so that everything was transformed into something precious. Even straw. It never turned to gold again after those three enchanted nights, no matter how long I sat at the wheel and how fast I span, which is why my husband the king saw past my regal dresses of cloth of gold to the plain miller's daughter beneath, and spurned me. It has long been his belief that he was tricked into marriage, but he wed me with all ceremony before his court, and he cannot put me aside.

I do not miss my looks. They are gone, and that is all. They bought me riches but they never brought me joy. I do not deserve joy: a man helped me, and I betrayed him, and he died. Everything has its price. But I am rich, and there are some consolations. My family will never go hungry now, and my sisters did not have to trade their bodies for security with men who did not love them, or please them: I made sure of that. I have my son, although I mourn his father's absence, because for all that I was a foolish, vain and frightened girl, there was love there, too. My husband lets me keep my son close by, and prefers that the court does not see him. This is on account of his stature. He has never attained a height much beyond that of a child.

He grew into the spitting image of his father and I never say his name aloud.

TZEITEL'S HEARTS

Tzeitel had three hearts but only two beat in her body. The other was locked in a bone chest.

Many years before, Tzeitel met a man. One of her hearts had quivered and fluttered and when it seemed the man loved Tzeitel back, the heart grew wings and flew out of her chest to be with him. For a while, the man's heart and Tzeitel's heart soared in tandem, but then the man saw that his future lay somewhere that wasn't with Tzeitel, so he took back his heart and went off to fulfill his destiny. And Tzeitel's heart, which had beat so hard with love and hope, shriveled and dried up, and made its way back to Tzeitel.

When she tried to replace it in her bosom it was too painful to bear, so she bathed it in tears and

because it was too broken to mend, locked it safely in the bone chest where no further hurt could come to it. Then she told herself that even if one heart was unwanted, she had two other hearts, and the rest of her life to live.

It may seem out of the everyday way to have more than one heart, but like her mother and her grandmother and many, many ancestors going back to the days when Baba Yaga rode her cauldron over the Carpathians, Tzeitel was a witch. She didn't make a song and dance act about it and draw attention to herself. She knew the history of her kind: the burning times and the drowning times. She knew that there were people who would hurt her if they found out what it was about her that made her different. But blood will out. Tzeitel was a witch, and even though she kept herself to herself, there was no getting away from it.

She lived in a higgledy-piggledy shed piled up with wobbly towers of books and charms and knick-knacks and frocks and scraps of fabric. When she wasn't in public, she dressed in raggy scraps and shredded layers of odds and ends and her hair looked as if it had been chewed by rats. Her windowsill was bushy with herbs that she grew in jam jars and coffee containers. Inside, on her single gas ring, a cauldron bubbled and boiled with potions that she put into bottles and jars that she adorned with a neatly written label with her trade

name, Tzeitel's Remedies, and a one-line description of the contents.

Every weekend she dressed in a neat black dress and sold her remedies on a table covered in a chenille bedspread at the local farmers' market. There were potions to make skin softer, and potions to make wrinkles disappear, and potions to make even the frizziest hair smooth and soft. The potions were a good price, and they worked, too, which meant people came back. And regular customers knew that if they asked nicely, when no-one else was in earshot, Tzeitel could be asked to make other potions, too.

Even though it was good for business, it worried Tzeitel that her clients were so anxious about their faces. 'Make me look flawless,' they'd beg her, in whispers, as if the faint lines on their faces were deep scars on the tissue of their souls. 'Make me look young,' they'd plead, desperate to conceal the impressions made by a lifetime of living, loving, laughing and crying. 'Make me look like you,' they'd implore, and Tzeitel would do a quick double-take before realising that she'd applied her own products to make herself nice for a public appearance, and that yes, they worked very well indeed.

'Make my nose smaller,' the customers would ask her. 'Make my lips bigger.' 'Make my forehead smooth.' And Tzeitel would do what she could, because one of her remaining hearts was filled with love for humankind and she hated to see how unhappy her customers were made by their own faces. But there were some things she couldn't remedy, no matter how much her customers wanted her to. 'Make my eyes a different colour.' 'Give me cheekbones like knives.' 'Change the shape of my face.' 'Make me into someone else.' Even if her powers had allowed her, she preferred to work with nature rather than against it, and anyway she thought their faces were beautiful, scored with the stories of the lives they had lived. Unlike her customers, whose thoughts had been muddied by too many magazine articles that told them what was wrong with them, she had been gifted with the ability to see things clearly.

Not one of them asked her to help them to like themselves more, and this made her sad. It was a relief to get home, where she could take off the black dress, and put the public image in the box under the bed where she kept useful spells and other, secret things, and go back to being her scratty, scruffy, comfortable self.

Tzeitel shared her life with Murgatroyd and his sister Mehitabel, who turned up three years ago and fooled her into thinking they were ordinary black cats such as any self-respecting witch would be happy to own. Once they got their paws under the table though, and decided that they'd like to stay with Tzeitel, who fed them generously, talked to them kindly and let them sleep with her in her wrought iron bed, they dropped their disguise, shedding their cloak of blackness to reveal themselves in their true colours.

As their bodies became lighter and lighter, a pair of magical Siamese emerged. Murgatroyd kept his

black face, black paws and black tail, and Mehitabel faded even further, until all that was left of her dark disguise was a furry brown pansy face and paws the colour of chocolate pralines.

'They have the same skill that I do,' thought a delighted Tzeitel. 'They can alter their appearance so they blend in, in the outside world. But whereas my real self, the one I keep for my private life, is less conventionally beautiful than the one I use for show, Murgatroyd and Mehitabel only reveal their true beauty when they are completely at home. To win the trust of an animal truly is a magical thing.' She'd never seen anything so enchanting and as something in her bosom throbbed and fluttered, she realised that the furry pair had stolen her third heart.

'Mow,' noted Mehitabel in soft agreement. She was a thoughtful little cat. 'Wah,' said Murgatroyd, at the top of his voice, but that was because he was thinking about chicken. Although they were extravagantly gorgeous, neither of them worried about what they looked like. It never crossed their minds. They had better things to think about. Murgatroyd worried about food, and Mehitabel worried about Murgatroyd, licking the insides of his ears to calm him down when he got himself worked up about things.

The three of them lived very happily together in their wonky shed, and it never occurred to Tzeitel, who kept herself busy trying to help her clients with their distressing problems, that there might be anything that could improve the quality of her life.

'If I added the tincture of violets that I prepared last Beltane to the beeswax emulsion, that would calm skin irritation and ease heartbreak,' she decided. 'And violets help with loneliness too. I think some of my customers are more lonely than they will admit. And perhaps also a touch of red clover infusion, to increase confidence. Perhaps that would do the trick. What do you think, Mehitabel? Do you think I could put the price up? I need to put in an order for your food.'

'Mow,' said Mehitabel, wisely. And Tzeitel followed her advice, and made up the potion. And it worked. Sales increased, and Tzeitel had to put in extra hours searching for more violets. But instead of the cream making her clients happier, their demands increased.

'You're so clever. Do you think you could make me up something that would make my eyelashes come out to here, and at the same time, something that would make my ears slightly smaller? And I've heard small pink nipples are considered much more chic than big brown ones. I don't suppose you…?'

It upset Tzeitel that it was not within her powers to make her poor clients happy, but she was a realist and understood that each witch has her own gift, and that not all things are possible, even in the world of magic. She had a friend, for instance, who had beautiful lacquered fingernails. Shooting sparks from them was a fantastic party piece but there weren't many real-world applications, especially since most people had stopped smoking. At least one of her gifts was useful, even if the other one – the gift of seeing what was in front of her – didn't improve the quality of anyone's lives, not even hers. It was frustrating, seeing how lovely her clients were, inside and out, and not being able to make them see it too.

And then, one day as Tzeitel was lying on her bed wondering how she could create a potion that would make her clients look in the mirror and see what she saw in them, she heard the music.

It was very faint, and faraway, and it was a tune unlike any she'd ever heard, except in her imagination. It was part waltz, part fanfare. A wonky, plinky, plonky tune, which trickled into her ears and took hold of her imagination. Bells pinged. Tingalingaling. As it got louder, it made her toes tap. She realised she was grinning from ear to ear. Gently pushing Murgatroyd and Mehitabel from their cosy resting places along her outstretched legs, she wriggled herself upright, and made her way to the door.

The cats accompanied her, cross about being disturbed and curious to know what was going on. 'Wah,' complained Murgatroyd. 'Mow,' agreed Mehitabel. They were united in deep suspicion of the unknown. By the time Tzeitel opened the door, two black cats stood just behind her.

The music came from the most extraordinary contraption Tzeitel had ever seen: a mechanical piano, mounted on an antique pram frame and surmounted with a great golden phonograph horn. As the captivating tune got louder and louder, and the contraption came nearer and nearer, Tzeitel found herself first marking out a little dance, and then, throwing all propriety to the winds, kicking up her skirts and showing her striped socks as she gavotted wildly in the street.

Eventually the music came to a stop, and so did Tzeitel. She was flushed, and her hair was a mess, but she didn't care. She was out of breath, and giddy, and as happy as she could ever remember being.

It took her a moment to remember her manners, and look round to see who had made the marvellous music, so she could thank them. And at first she couldn't see anything. But then a figure, every bit as extraordinary as his instrument, stepped out from behind the big golden horn. He had an eye patch, and a wooden leg, and a parrot sitting on his shoulder, which lifted its great grey wings as he bowed to Tzeitel.

'Did you like it, then?' His weathered face cracked in a hundred places as he smiled the widest smile Tzeitel had ever seen. The bright blue eye that wasn't covered by an eye patch twinkled like electricity. Tzeitel's own eyes, which were brown, glowed like lit coals in agreement.

'What is it?' She pointed at the contraption. 'And who are you?'

This time, the figure doffed his top hat to reveal that where its crown should be, there was a bunch of

flowers. He removed them deftly and waved them in the direction of his contraption before offering them to Tzeitel.

'That is a tingalary. And that makes me the Tingalary Man.'

Tingalary. Tzeitel smiled even more broadly, and as she took the flowers, she remembered her grandma telling her stories about the old days. The times when people lived in little dark cramped houses in little dark narrow alleys with one outside lavatory between eight houses, and everyone knowing each other's business. How the tingalary man would come and play tunes, and everyone, whatever they were doing, would leave their pokey little houses and come and dance in the street to the tunes they loved most. Lily of Laguna. I know she likes me, I know she likes me, because she said so. Daisy Daisy. Give me your answer do. I'm half crazy…

'Can you play any other songs?'

'Any song you like. If you fancy it, I'll play it. What might you have in mind?'

'Something funny. Can you play something funny?'

'For you, my dear, I can play down the stars. But if funny you want, funny you shall have.'

The Tingalary Man limped to the back of his tingalary and began to crank a handle that Tzeitel had not previously noticed. As he did, a chirpy refrain emanated from the horn, so inherently comical that it made Tzeitel stick out her elbows and do a silly walk. The Tingalary Man stepped out from behind the Tingalary and despite his limp, joined in, dancing with his knees in the air. The real knee went up of its own accord and the wooden one because the Tingalary Man pulled on a string attached to it in much the same manner as a puppeteer.

'Oh what a palaver,' he sang in perfect Cockney. 'Never been so annoyed in all me life.'

Tzeitel laughed so much she had to sit on the floor. When she looked up, through streaming eyes, she could see Murgatroyd and Mehitabel's eyes, four indignant sapphires, glowering at her as if she'd lost her wits. She poked out her tongue at them and turned back to the Tingalary Man. And then, because seeing what was in front of her was one of her witch-talents, she noticed that beneath his kindly manner and twinkling eyes, the Tingalary Man was in pain, and tired, and hungry, not just for food but a friendly soul to pass the time of day with him.

'Does it hurt?' she asked.

'It does lass, and the one that's missing too, which is an odd thing, though I've got used to it. But it's hard work pushing that thing about, day in day out, and me being lopsided doesn't help. But I've got songs, and people need songs, so off to work I go. Hey ho.' He grimaced wryly, and the great grey parrot raised its wings in the air. 'Mucky house,' it squawked. 'What a mess.'

'Manners,' admonished the Tingalary Man, and the parrot settled down.

'It is a bit of a mess.' Tzeitel always had better things to do than housework, and often wished she could just waft a wand around, but her Mother had told her very sternly that she could use her powers in that direction if that was what she really wanted, but that would leave her with less energy to expend in other areas. 'It is clean though. And I made some curry earlier on. Chick pea and spinach. It's not bad. Would you like a plate?'

The Tingalary Man gave her an appreciative nod, so Tzeitel went inside to fetch it. Murgatroyd and Mehitabel, the colour of coal, vanished into the shadows so only their blue eyes were visible.

'I know you don't like strangers, but honestly. You could come out and say hello.'

'Wah' said Murgatroyd. Murgatroyd was willing to defend his home and his loved ones from intruders. 'Mow,' said Mehitabel. She worried that strangers might take her away, and made herself scarce whilst Tzeitel warmed up the curry. Murgatroyd sat on windowsill and watched intently. 'I can't turn it into chicken,' Tzeitel told him. 'You'll just have to wait.'

Sitting on the step, the Tingalary Man wolfed his plateful once it was warmed up, and by way of thanks, limped round to the back of his tingalary to show Tzeitel its insides. 'See that barrel? Each of those pins is a short note, and the staples are the longer notes – if you look closely, they're different lengths. And then when I turn the barrel round – like so,' and he cranked the handle, 'that's where the music comes from.'

'But surely each song is a different pattern?'

'In general, yes.' The Tingalary Man winked his good eye.

'So you need a new pattern for each tune you play?'

'Tends to be that way, with barrel organs.' He winked again, and cranked the handle. As the handful of notes plinked out, Tzeitel's feet found themselves a-tapping.

'But you said earlier you could play anything I liked.'

'So I did. And so I can. But as for the hows and whys of it, that would be telling.' He winked again, and smiled, and Tzeitel found herself smiling back. She knew about hows and whys and not telling. 'And now I must be on my way.' He doffed his hat again, then turned around and set to work.

Tzeitel watched him, limping as he pushed the heavy tingalary, until he was first a silhouetted figure with the parrot on his shoulder, then a speck, and then vanished into the distance. Then she went inside.

'Wah.' Murgatroyd jumped on the windowsill and humped his back against her hand. As she stroked him, his blackness faded into creamy brown fur everywhere except for his mask, paws and tail. Tzeitel kissed the top of his silky head and stroked his velvet ears.

'You really are handsome. Chicken?'

'Wah.'

'Do you think your sister will come out? Mehitabel?'

Mehitabel poked out her nose from under the bed, but it took her hours before she decided to stop being a black cat and show her true colours. And Tzeitel, when she went back to what she had been doing earlier, found that the Tingalary Man's tune had wormed its way into her ears and kept insisting on replaying itself in her head, and that every time it did, her face began to smile and her feet started to dance.

The little tune went round and round in her head for some time. Tzeitel walked around with a lighter step than usual, and chose brightly patterned socks to wear in place of her usual striped ones. She found herself humming the tune, and noticed that as she did, Murgatroyd and Mehitabel twitched the tips of their tails in time to her humming.

'You see? There was nothing to be scared of, was there? Just a funny man with a funny instrument that played nice tunes.'

'Mow,' said Mehitabel agreeably. 'Wah,' chimed Murgatroyd. And Tzeitel, wondering if she kept herself to herself just a little too much, made an excuse to herself about needing to go for a walk to find some more ingredients, but although she found violet and beeswax and orange flower water, no matter how hard she looked, there was no sign of a barrel organ on a pram-base being pushed by a rickety gentleman with a parrot and a limp. Tzeitel took her packages home, got out her trusty bowls and pans to cook up the ingredients into a new batch of brightening face cream, and glanced down at her feet. Her socks, covered in a bright pattern of hearts and flowers, suddenly annoyed her. Ripping them off, she rolled them in a ball and hurled them onto the bed. The balled up socks landed where the cats were nesting in old feather quilts.

'Wah!' objected Murgatroyd, springing up in alarm. 'Wah, wah,' echoed Mehitabel, who scuttled under the bed.

'I'm sorry, I'm sorry.' Tzeitel abandoned her potion to apologise to the cats. 'I don't know what's the matter with me.' By the time she got back to her pots the mixture had congealed into a lumpy mess. Tzeitel hated waste so she heated it up again, added some rosewater and witch hazel and beat it with a whisk until it was smooth. Then she decanted it into pots and quickly labelled them. Vanishing cream. Some of her clients had been specifically asking for vanishing cream. But there was an ingredient missing, and she couldn't, for the life of her, remember what it was.

'Tomorrow's the farmer's market and if I don't take the new batch I'll be short of stock,' she worried. 'I hope it rains and no-one turns up.'

But it was sunny that weekend, and again the weekend after, which meant Tzeitel was kept busy fulfilling orders and making new stock, and gradually, the funny little tune faded from her mind and she settled back into her routine. And Murgatroyd and Mehitabel persuaded her to grow some nice fresh catnip, and then made her laugh by rolling in it when she sprinkled the leaves on the eiderdowns on top of the big wrought iron bed.

The following weekend, though, she had an altercation on her hands. The batch of vanishing cream had sold out the previous week, and some customers turned up especially to complain about the results. 'I've still got freckles,' grumbled one of them. 'I put it on every night before bed, just as you said, and they're still there.' 'My wrinkles are as bad as ever,' complained another. 'And the lines round my mouth are worse than ever.' You should give up smoking and snarking if you don't want a cat's bum mouth,' thought Tzeitel, but she didn't say anything, because the customer is always right.

When people saw that Tzeitel's customers were grumbling, more weighed in. 'I put it on my back fat and it's still there,' huffed one of them. 'What are you going to do about it?' "I rubbed it into my saddlebags and they didn't vanish either,' said another one. 'I asked you if it would make me look younger and I was expecting 20 years to vanish,' grumbled someone else. 'It's all false pretense if you ask me.'

Tzeitel looked round at their tetchy, discontented faces. She understood that the customers she had treated with love and kindness had turned on her and the heart that cared for them started to ache. 'I'm sorry,' she muttered. 'I was only trying to help.'

'It's just not good enough,' retaliated the woman with the cat's bum mouth. She pushed her face forward so Tzeitel could smell her stale breath. There was no kindness in her eyes. 'I always thought there was something not quite right about you.'

Like a flash. This is how it starts, thought Tzeitel, and although it had never happened to her, she had been brought up with the stories. This is how it has always began, when they have asked us for things that we cannot do and they believe we have failed them, and it ends in my kind being searched and stripped and swum and scratched, dunked and dipped and pricked. Fear prickled along the length of her spine, and the faces around her pressed in, crosser and crosser, closer and closer.

Then she heard it over the – a very faint, but distinctly winky, wonky, plinky plonky tune. Tzeitel's persecutors heard it too, and as the sound came nearer, they paused in haranguing her and lifted their heads to make out the music more clearly. Some of their eyes lit up in hope, and the corners of some of their lips began to twitch. As the tune came nearer still, the angry customers moved towards it, turning round just as the Tingalary Man appeared round the corner, parrot on his shoulder, pushing his barrel organ as the notes of the jauntiest polka that had ever been played trumpeted out of the barrel organ's great golden horn.

As one, Tzeitel's customers forget how angry they were and began to dance. One-two-three-hop, one-two-three-hop, round and round, showing their knees with great big smiles on their faces, as the Tingalary Man made his way to Tzeitel's table.

'Hop on,' he yelled.

Tzeitel managed to bundle her unsold potions into her basket, but she was too shaken to say anything as the Tingalary Man handed her onto the pram frame. He gave the ladies a burst of a fast mazurka so that they danced themselves out of breath, then turned to Tzeitel. 'They've danced themselves inside out. Won't remember a thing tomorrow. Right. Let's get you home.'

He set off at such a cracking pace that the wind whistled through Tzeitel's hair. She watched the gallant figure of the Tingalary Man, putting his best foot forward and then his wooden one, pushing his pram base and cranking the handle of his barrel organ, and found her feet trying to tap out the tune. There was something familiar about it. Something that reminded her of her mother, and her grandmother, and made her feel warm inside. They were getting near to Tzeitel's house when she realised what the Tingalary Man was playing.

'Daisy, daisy.' She remembered her Grandmother singing that to her. 'Give me your answer do.' A little smile crept across her face as she looked at her rescuer, barreling along on his good leg and his wooden one, with his one blue eye glinting with kindness and the parrot sitting on his shoulder using its great grey wings to steady itself when there were bumps in the road.

'In you get.' The Tingalary Man parked his Tingalary outside Tzeitel's shack and ushered her in. 'In there.' He pointed to the big wrought iron bed. 'You've had a bit of a shock. Let's wrap you up in a blanket.' Murgatroyd and Mehitabel, who had turned black, went to sit on the side of the bed that was furthest from the Tingalary Man and his parrot.

'Oh don't be silly,' he said. 'Go sit on your mum.'

'Mow.' Mehitabel wasn't convinced, but 'wah', said Murgatroyd, and when he jumped up on the bed to sit on Tzeitel, Mehitabel hopped up and tucked herself under Tzeitel's arm, and behind her brother, where no one could see her.

'That's more like it.' The Tingalary Man nodded in approval, and the parrot squawked and plucked a bit of lint off the Tingalary Man's jacket.

'You go sit on the headboard, it's just right for a perch for an old grey parrot.' The Tingalary Man rolled his shoulder as the parrot flew off to do as it had been told.

Then he limped over to the gas ring. 'No kettle?' Unperturbed, he set the cauldron to boil. 'Nice cup of tea and you'll be right as rain. No-one makes a better cup of tea than I do.'

Wrapped up like a chrysalis in her blanket, Tzeitel found herself smiling.

'Where did you learn that then?"

'When I was at sea.'

'Were you a sailor?'

'I used to be a pirate captain, but I kept getting seasick. Still walk with a roll though.' The kettle boiled and he carefully stirred two enamel mugs, then carried them over to Tzeitel. There was nowhere to sit down when he'd given her a mug, so he propped himself against the wall to drink his.

'You can sit here.' Tzeitel wriggled half out of her blanket and patted the bed next to her. 'There's plenty of room.'

So the Tingalary Man sat down next to her, and as they drank their tea, he told her about the ups and downs of life on the ocean waves, and the great battles he'd fought, and the run-ins he'd had, and the injuries he'd suffered, and then he sung her some sea shanties and made light of his losses.

'There's not much left of me,' said the Tingalary Man. 'I'm half the man I used to be.'

'Half of you is better than most people. Look what you can do. You did what I've never been able to manage with my customers. You made them happy. It's better than magic.'

'I don't know about magic. I made them forget about themselves, which is halfway to happiness if you ask me.'

He looked thoughtful for a minute and rubbed his hand along his wooden leg.

'I was a bit of a bad lot so what's left it is the best of me,' he offered after a moment. 'But I make the most of what I've got. There's more than enough badness in the world without me adding to it. It's a weight off to be rid of it.' He wriggled about, and pulled a face. 'Even if it does give me a right old twinge.'

As he spoke, Tzeitel stroked Murgatroyd and Mehitabel with the hand that wasn't holding the tea, and their black fur faded so that they looked like a pair of Siamese twins again.

As their fur lightened, though, the sky darkened, and night began to fall, and Tzeitel's eyelids began to droop. She looked at Mehitabel and Murgatroyd, who had fallen asleep nose-to-nose with their paws around each other, and then she looked at the parrot, who had tucked his head under his wing and was snoring softly. And then she looked at the Tingalary Man, who had spirited her away from the cross customers and taken care of her and made her warm with laughter, and she saw that although his body was broken, he had the kindest spirit she had ever met.

'You can sleep here if you like.'

'I might just do that,' said the Tingalary Man. He unstrapped his leg, and stretched himself out next to her and covered himself with half of the blanket. 'Want a cuddle?' So Tzeitel fitted herself into the space where half of his body was missing, and then Murgatroyd and Mehitabel woke up and tucked themselves under the blanket so they were curled up on top of Tzeitel and the Tingalary Man. The parrot woke up too, and moving to settle himself on the Tingalary Man's shoulder, put his head under his wing again. And they all went to sleep in a pile.

And very, very faintly, Tzeitel, who kept drifting in and out of sleep, heard a knocking. It came from under the bed. She didn't want to hear it at first, and tried to block it out, but although it was very soft, it was also very persistent. And Tzeitel, who had almost forgotten it was there because it was so long ago that she had locked it away in a bone chest, looked at the Tingalary Man and realised that it was her third heart, and that it had been mended, and that the time had come for her to put it back in her chest again.

And the knocking got louder, so that Tzeitel was sure it would wake up the sleeping man and cats and parrots, and then it got louder still, so that it was a great banging and a beating that rattled the bed and jerked it in its frame so that everyone in it sat bolt upright. Then the heart burst out from its bone chest and fluttered up into the room, unsteady in its flight at first and then smoother and stronger. And the grey parrot spread his wings and flew up to the heart, and together they danced in a winged duet round the room, dipping and diving, soaring and wheeling, as Tzeitel and the Tingalary Man and Murgatroyd and Mehitabel watched in wide-eyed wonder. And then when they had exhausted themselves, the heart and the parrot gently glided down to join everyone. The parrot settled on the Tingalary Man's shoulder and tucked its head under its wing. The heart slotted itself quietly back into Tzeitel's bosom where it belonged. And everyone folded themselves into each other, and settled down, and went back to sleep.

DUCK BUTTER AND GHERKIN JUICE

The 1960s and '70s underground rock scene has yielded may strange tales of excess and out-there voyaging, but none are more bizarre than the stories told around the epic lost album *Duck Butter and Gherkin Juice* by enigmatic legend Captain C.

'Some trip out there' t-shirts are this year's hot festival fashion accessory, but behind the retro graphics is a mystery that has become part of pop cultural folklore. Anyone who was present at the remarkable sessions that produced *Duck Butter and Gherkin Juice*, or who heard out-takes, knows they listened to something extraordinary. Tracks that have emerged – *Aubergine, Codeine, Appalling Pauline* and *The Ballad of Captain C and Mama T* being outstanding examples – show a musician at the height of extraordinary powers. The build-up to the album was phenomenal, with international tour dates sold out, headline slots at festivals eagerly awaited and magazine covers secured. The buzz on the underground grapevine was that Captain C had produced an era-defining masterpiece.

And yet *Duck Butter and Gherkin Juice* was never released. In the small hours after the day that recording was completed, on 16 October 1971, Captain C absconded with the master tapes and to all extents and purposes, vanished off the face of the earth.

Way before *Duck Butter and Gherkin Juice*, Captain C was one of the London freak scene's most charismatic leading lights. A flamboyant black-clad individual with a mane of piratical black curls and luminous blue eyes daubed in kohl, he had come out of the London happening scene kicking and screaming with his first offering, *Tiger Tank*, an abrasive psychedelic exploration of the horrors of war delivered in a baritone croon alternatively seductive and menacing. Its follow-up, *Arkham Asylum*, a musical journey into the realms of excess and insanity, cemented his position as a transgressive figurehead for a counterculture interested in finding its way as far out there as possible.

Wild and crazy characters populated the scene, but none more so than Captain C. 'Captain C was way out there,' remembers scenester and sometimes musical sidekick Roger, known as 'The Cabin Boy'. 'He was one of those cats you don't meet that often – and when you do, they leave a helluva impression. All the dudes wanted to be him, and the chicks – they couldn't get enough of him.' A superb raconteur and a gregarious host, Captain C drew attention like a magnet, and his creativity went beyond the music scene to encompass successful forays into poetry, screenplays, filmmaking, acting and art. But there were suggestions of a darker side, too. Rumours abounded of gangland connections, bare-knuckle fighting, car park brawling and accidental overdoses. It was suggested that he had abducted his common-law wife, Mama, from a circus sideshow where she had danced and told fortunes and he had performed a specialty act for adult audiences as The Great Bummo. It all added to the mystique of this underworld adventurer.

Global success for *Arkham Asylum* had brought with it the privileges of stardom, including private jets, trashing hotel suites, limos and a blank slate from the record company to do whatever Captain C wanted, with no consideration of the cost. After the last leg of the *Arkham Asylum* tour, though, Captain C provoked an industry-wide reaction as he and Mama checked out of the Chateau Marmont with their possessions in a wheelbarrow. 'We're going into the desert,' he told stunned reporters. 'We're going to meet the sun.' It was the last anyone heard of him for three months.

When he returned, lean, wiry and sunburnt, he set to work with furious energy with plans for an ambitious double album. 'It's going to be about everything – sex, the cosmos and the god that's in in all of us,' he pronounced. 'We've had some trip out there. We've seen how it's all connected.' His star was riding so high that he could do what he wanted, and he took full advantage. *Duck Butter and Gherkin Juice* sessions took place in The Great Pyramid at Giza, at Bran Castle in Transylvania, at Abbey Road and in Muscle Shoals, where a gospel choir was on hand on a 24-hour rota to fit in the eccentric musician's erratic recording schedule. Gnawa trance musicians were flown in from Morocco, voodoo priestesses from New Orleans, Sufis from Turkey and a Romanian wedding band occupied a suite at Chateau Marmont for four months as Captain C threaded their violin parts into his epic work in progress. Frank Zappa, David Bowie, Jim Morrison, John Lennon and Captain Beefheart all put in guest appearances. 'It's an honour to be part of it,' gushed Bowie. 'Everything I've done pales into insignificance next to this.'

The word on the street was that this was to be the album not just of the year, but of the decade. The artwork was completed, the iconic 'Some trip out there' t-shirts printed, the music writers slavering over any gnostic comment Captain C deigned to thrown their way.

And the night he finished the final session, he picked up the tapes, put them in a supermarket carrier bag, walked out of the studio with Mama and was never seen again.

A week after he failed to return, there was an outcry. A missing person's report was filed, and police investigations carried out worldwide. The world's press sent investigate reporters to track down the missing superstar and try to put together the pieces of events leading up to his disappearance. Every possible lead was followed up, including an unidentifiable carcass nibbled to death by koi carp in an ornamental pond at a stately home in Nether Barton, but the mystery has never been solved. The millions of pounds poured by the record company into the project have never been successfully accounted for.

Inevitably, tall tales and conspiracy theories abounded, ranging from the wacked-out 'abducted by aliens' and the notion that his disappearance was in some way connected to shamanic training undertaken whilst he was in the desert to the plausible, or even possible: his East End connections had caught up with him; he'd returned with Mama to the life of an anonymous travelling circus performer; he had resurfaced in the 1980s as the inaccessible head honcho of the cult psych-drone-rock record label SumDaze.

One-time sidekick Roger "The Cabin Boy' takes all this with a pinch of salt. 'What you have to remember about the Captain was he always a step ahead. Whatever anyone thought he'd do, he'd already gone beyond. Everyone thinks it was madness, but whatever he did, there was a method to it.'

Occasional reports of possible sightings have only fanned the flames of interest. Captain C has reputedly been spotted at a quiz night in a small village in Northampton, lurking in a graveyard in Leeds, staring at a shelf of gherkins in Lidl and looking disinterested at an Adam Ant concert in Oxford. In 2006, Canongate Books paid a £1 million advance for a collection of anonymously submitted short stories, each one of which had the title of a *Duck Butter and Gherkin Juice* song, but the former members of the KLF subsequently admitted they had compiled the collection as an art prank, and used the advance to buy all the copies of the book, which they then burned.

The most recent sighting involves a fuzzy 17-second YouTube clip, shot on a smartphone, of a couple resembling Captain C and Mama in Western Favell, a shopping mall on the outskirts of Northampton. In it, the couple are standing at the pharmacy counter, peering intently at the codeine-based over-the-counter medications. The clip has been cut with footage from the famous Stones in the Park gig. Even in the company of the cream of London's beautiful people and the world's most famous rock stars, Captain C and a cheesecloth-swathed Mama have the aura of being set apart. The camera pans to Mick Jagger. 'You want to know who really made it all the way out there?' Jagger points to Captain C, a looming shadow in tight black loons and t-shirt next to the dandified Rolling Stone in his frilly white blouse. 'This cat, man. He's off the map. He's gone further out there than anyone.'

Perhaps Jagger, whose role as Turner in the film *Performance* was said by some to be directly influenced by his meetings with Captain C, was more prophetic than he knew. A shopping mall in the middle of nowhere might seem an anti-climactic scenario for a star who shone so brightly that his fans would have preferred him to crash and burn, like a latter-day Icarus. But perhaps Captain C, wherever he is, having created not just a record but the stuff of legend, is somewhere out there, further than anyone else has ever been, still living on the record company's unaccounted millions, and having the last laugh.

HOMING

She gazes out of the train window and looks for birds.

She used to stand and watch the birds through a square of glass with cream-painted bars. How lovely it would be to see them now. The small, gentle, brown birds, singing their simple, cheerful songs. The sparrows and the thrushes. Not the magpies. She never liked the magpies. The way they bullied the smaller birds. But Susan has told her there will be other birds.

Susan is talking through the glass, though the rumbling engine means she has to lip-read. 'Don't forget. Liverpool Street. You need to change at Liverpool Street.'

She nods. 'Liverpool Street. I need to change at Liverpool Street.' She mouths the words back, but her mind is scanning through the birds she might see when she gets to Hannah's. Thrush. Blackbird. Owl. That would be a thing, to see an owl. That silent swoop of feathers. You could feel it in the air without hearing a thing. She wonders if there might be owls, in Macclesfield.

'Don't forget your case,' mouths Susan. She had forgotten about the case, on the seat next to her, but she pats it to reassure Susan. She pats it until the train pulls out, and she can no longer see Susan, waving. And then she watches from the window and hopes for a glimpse of wings in flight.

The only birds she sees are pigeons. Some people think they're vermin, but it's not their fault they're scruffy and horrible. They're just trying to live their lives. Feed their families.

Families, she thinks. I am going to Hannah in Macclesfield. She is my family and she has a family of her own, who will be my family too, though I have never met them. I have seen their photographs. Hannah, Robbie and Sean. Hannah brought pictures so Sarah could see them growing up. 'I'm a nanna,' she'd say proudly after Hannah had gone. If it were Susan she'd show the pictures too, but not the other nurses. Sarah wonders if Susan will be there when the train gets to Liverpool Street.

Each time the train stops, more people get on. All the seats are taken. She has to move her case onto the floor. Hannah, Robbie and Sean. She sings the words under her breath so that the notes of the names become a soft, chirruping sound. And then the train is swallowed up by the tunnel of the underground, engulfing her in great, terrifying darkness so that she barely knows what to do with herself. 'Hannahrobbieandsean,' she thinks, 'hannahrobbieandsean,' and rocks, just slightly. Enough to soothe herself but not so that other people notice.

By the time the train pulls into Liverpool Street, all she wants is to get away from the darkness and noise. She pushes her way to the exit. She is too quietly frantic to remember leaving her case behind. The only things she's thinking of are light, and air, and escape. The last thing on her mind is her daughter and the grandsons she has never met, who will be waiting, in a few hours, to collect her from the National Express coach station in Manchester.

Everyone is in a hurry. She has never seen so many people. The flutters are in her stomach but not as bad as they were on the train, and Susan always says that no one will help her if she can't tell them what the matter is. The first lady she approaches looks sensible and helpful but when she sees Sarah, she swerves. Although she is careful to be polite, the next lady looks at the space where she is standing as if nobody is there. She looks for another lady but there are only men. This makes the flutters stronger, almost a flapping inside her. Then there is another lady with a kind face.

'I need to change at Liverpool Street.'

'This is Liverpool Street. You're in the right place.' The lady gives her a firm, brisk smile that means she doesn't want to say anything else.

'I need to change at Liverpool Street.' The flapping is like a beating now, a great beating of wings inside her. She takes a very deep breath. Wraps her right arm over the beating, and then holds her right shoulder with her left hand. Wraps herself up. 'Hannahrobbieandsean,' she says.

'I'm sure they'll find you,' says the lady, not unkindly, but walking away as she is saying the words.

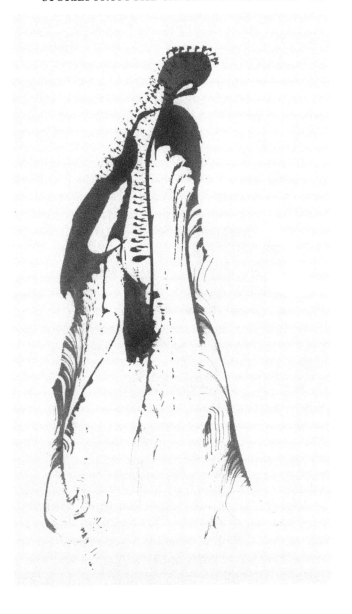

Then there's someone else, a younger woman, who puts a hand on her arm. Now the beating is so strong it needs to escape, and bursts out of her in a flurry of hissing and spitting, her arms flailing as she tries to bat the woman away from her. 'Get off me,' she squawks. 'Get off get off get off.' When she stops for breath, there is no young woman and the people are standing round her, with shocked faces. When she moves towards them, they move back, all together. She pushes her hands into the pockets of her brown coat, tucks her neck inside her collar, and sets off, looking at the floor, but not at the people.

She only stops walking when she sees the birds. Birds on steps, a lot of steps, very wide, going up to a big dome. Pigeons. She has never seen so many pigeons. She approaches them very softly, to get a better look, but not wanting to frighten them. The pigeons don't fly away. She moves closer, just a few inches, but still they don't fly. It's worth the risk just to get a little nearer. People say they are not nice but look at that one, the way it is picking up one pink foot so daintily, as if it were dancing. Look at the eyes of that one over there, like currants, but also shiny, like jet. She once went to Whitby. The shops were full of jet, carved into shapes. 'Morbid Victorian rubbish,' she remembers her father saying, in his big voice, which meant that she and her mam wouldn't dare say out loud that they thought it was pretty.

She moves by inches until she is right next to the pigeons, and still they don't fly away from her. Not like those ladies. What was it she wanted from the ladies? She isn't quite sure. There is so much to think about, with the pigeons, that there isn't room for anything else in her head. Listen to that one, cooing. She wonders what it is saying. She tilts her head at the pigeon. She could swear it looks back at her.

There are people sitting on the steps, nearer the edge, and she wonders if the pigeons would mind if she sat with them. She lowers herself very gently, so as not to frighten them, and arranges herself on the step. The pigeon that looked at her is still there. She has never been this close to a bird – and it is quite a big bird, much bigger than a sparrow or a robin, or even a thrush. The wings in her stomach begin to flutter again, but this time it is exciting, like being on a merry-go-round that's going too fast. Feeling very scared, and very brave, she holds out a finger.

She is sitting in her usual spot when she feels someone approaching. She is used to this, because people take her picture, and often they are polite and ask if it is OK, and give her money and things to help her feed the birds. But this person is closer than she likes, and a man, and the birds don't like it either, because they are backing away.

'Not so near,' she whispers. It makes her happy that she can be fierce for the birds.

The man moves far enough away for Sarah not to mind him being there, so she looks at him. He is only small, and she likes his colourful clothes,

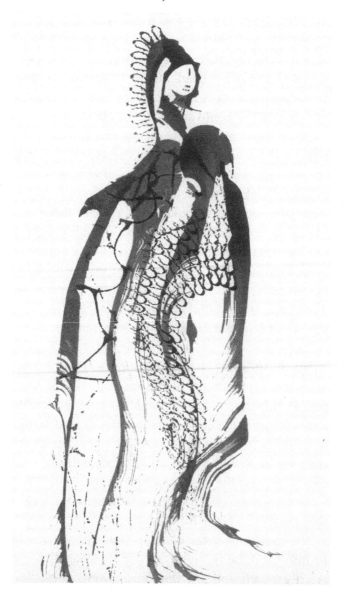

even if they are a bit dirty. But then she supposes her clothes must be a bit dirty too, quite a bit dirty by now, so maybe she and the man have something in common. She likes his hair, too, or what she can see of it under his woolly red cap. It is springy and curly, as if it is trying to fly away from his head, and although it is quite grey, she can see flecks of brown in it. Like the underneath of a thrush's wing.

He raises a McDonalds milkshake carton in her direction. She can hear the chink of coins, and she sees the man has got a box, all folded up but with its insides on the outside. It's got piano keys. Sarah knows this is a musical instrument but she can't remember its name.

'Hey. Like your birds, man,' he says. His face is wrinkled round the eyes, and he's got a wide smile. A lot of his teeth have fallen out. She doesn't want to wave at him in case it disturbs Robbie, who is on her shoulder with his head under his wing, and she can't nod because Sean is nesting on her hat and he wouldn't like it, and she mustn't smile because she doesn't know who this man is. But she doesn't think he means any harm, so she winks at him.

He comes back the next day, and gives her a few pounds out of his McDonalds carton. 'Not done badly today, the old hurdy-gurdy man.' The lines round his mouth make his smile even wider. 'Tuppence a bag, eh?' He seems perfectly happy to sit there quietly, smoking roll-ups and looking at the birds. She is quite pleased to see him when he comes back the next day, and the day after that. On the fifth day, she pats the step next to her.

'Perhaps if you keep still a bird will sit on you.' She doesn't know where the words came from, but when she thinks about it she is not sorry that she said them.

'Now there would be a thing.' He sits nice and still but the birds stay where they are. His face looks quite sad and Sarah feels sorry for him. It is the bravest she has ever been and she doesn't know what has come over her but she does it anyway: leans over and sprinkles some breadcrumbs on him. When the pigeon pecks it off him, then perches on his knee, he can't wipe the smile off his face. He huffs and goes pink and has to wipe his eye.

'I saw these green parrots, in Richmond Park,' he says, tilting his head this way and that. 'Blew my mind. I mean, green parrots. It was Hendrix. Hendrix let those parrots free. It changed me. Hendrix knew. You got to let a bird fly.'

She doesn't know what he's on about. Silly sausage.

'You know what they used to call me? Back in the day?' he says. She isn't really bothered. But it's bad manners not to answer questions when someone is talking to you.

'What did they call you?'

'Wazzo, man.' He's beaming, as if a light has been switched on inside him. His eyes are bright and shiny. Like currants, but also like jet. 'They used to call me Wazzo.'

What sort of name is that? Not a proper name, like Graham or Horace. She doesn't mind him being there, though, even when he blows his nose with a honk that makes Sean stand up on her head and flap his wings quite crossly. And if she comes to think about it, someone with such a silly name might not want to make other people's lives a misery. Pecking at you all the time. Peck peck peck.

They sit next to each other and the birds sit on them. Now there are two of them, people take more photographs, and leave money to buy things to help the birds. Help them too. Blankets now it's cold, and gloves.

They collect newspapers to sit on so the cold doesn't get into their bones, and sometimes she looks at the pictures. There is a woman who reminds her of someone, though she isn't sure who. Underneath it says she is confused and vulnerable, and her daughter is looking for her. She hopes she finds her family. It's important to be with your family. Sarah says the names of her family to sing herself to sleep before bedtime.

'Wazzorobbieandsean,' she chirps, pottering round in her speckled brown coat before she tucks herself up. 'Wazzorobbieandsean.' There's just enough room in their hidey-hole for the four of them, and she's stuffed rags and newspapers into the holes where the rain comes in. Wazzo brings back all sorts of bits and pieces that he finds, and she's got it quite comfy. Sarah's rather house-proud, now she's got her own nest.

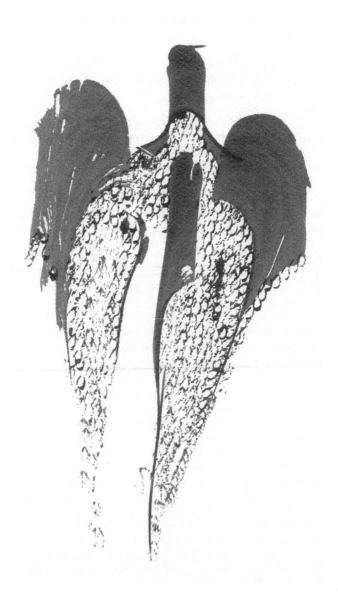

ACKNOWLEDGEMENTS

Thank you Harry Markos for believing in these stories and wanting a book.

Thank you Andi for your beautiful illustrations. Working with you on this has been a joy.

Thank you Ian Sharman for such a fantastic cover design, and Nathan Ward for his wonderful work-in-progress cover.

Thank you Chris Bradshaw for your love and faith. This book would not have happened without you, and is for you.

Thank you to the people who in many and wonderful ways inspired me and helped this book along the way: Everyone from Dancers Bizarre, past and present; Maria Woods; Michaela Noonan; Kirstin Ramskir; Jane Cornwell, Pete Valente and Sabrina Barlow, Julia Bell; Adam Macqueen and Michael Tierney; Maureen Cromey and Eve Ruxton-Cromey, Stephen Chamberlain and Sarah Woodley; Andrew Davies; Matthew Collin; Mike Power; Nick Triplow; Jilly Wosskow; Anni Swinburn; Frances Leviston; Storm; Sylvia Shatwell; Naomi Filmer; Jon and Elaine Price; Jonathan Telfer and Bex Bardon; Helena Orientale; Simona Jovic.

Thank you to my mother Patricia Jackson and my brother Marc Jackson. Also to Penny, Claude, Nellie and Teddy, whose pawprints are all over this.

Versions of some of the stories have been previously published: *Good Journey* in *Tell Tales lll*, *Rats in the Kitchen* in *Strictly Casual*, *Johnny Doll* in *Rocktext*, *Hooping the Girl* in *Standard Issue Magazine* and *Into the Blue* in *The Big Issue*. For this, thank you Julia Bell, Nii Ayikwei Parkes, Amy Prior, Ross Sutherland, Michaela Noonan and Becky Gardiner.

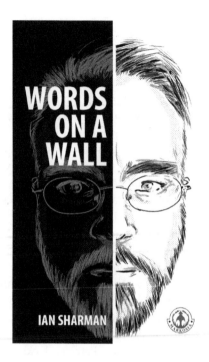

WORDS ON A WALL

Monsters, cryogenics, relationships, religion, war, dragons, cannibalism, angels, demons, space exploration, aliens, beans, eyes, traffic cones, gods, Chicago, pot plants, robots, a dive bar on Mars, goblins, heart break, July, cake, bees, geese, peacock flavour crisps and time travel are just some of the things you'll find in this eclectic collection of flash fiction and poetry. At times incredibly dark and deeply personal but often very, very silly.

ISBN: 978-1-911243-63-2

ALSO AVAILABLE FROM MARKOSIA

DORIAN GRAY

High school junior Dorian Gray lives a life of total excess. But when he receives his great-grandfather's portrait and journal, Dorian finds himself in the middle of the ultimate battle of good vs. evil. Now Dorian must put all his fears aside and figure out whom he can really trust.

ISBN: 978-1-911243-63-2

ALSO AVAILABLE FROM MARKOSIA

SINBAD: ROGUE OF MARS

A prophecy foretells of a stranger from distant lands who will vanquish the false king. Eight years after the assassination of King Dadgar, his vile nephew, Adhkar, has usurped his throne and enslaved the Azurian people, igniting a violent civil war. Having sailed the seven seas, exploring unknown lands, fighting countless monsters and battling evil wizards, could Sinbad be the stranger of the prophecy, or will he merely be a pawn in Adhkar's bloody game?

ISBN: 978-1-911243-63-2

CPSIA information can be obtained
at www.ICGtesting.com
Printed in the USA
BVHW04s1149240918
528349BV00011B/49/P